TWICE THE
PLEASURE

TWICE THE PLEASURE
BISEXUAL WOMEN'S EROTICA

EDITED BY
RACHEL KRAMER BUSSEL

Published in the United States by Cleis Press, Inc., 2246 Sixth Street, Berkeley, California 94710.

Printed in the United States.
Cover design: Scott Idleman/Blink
Cover photograph: JJRD & Cristoph Rosenberger/Getty Images
Text design: Frank Wiedemann

First Edition.
10 9 8 7 6 5 4 3 2 1

Trade paper ISBN: 978-1-57344-924-3
E-book ISBN: 978-1-57344-941-0

Contents

INTRODUCTION: HOT BI BABES: A BOTH/AND APPROACH TO BISEXUALITY

Woody Allen once famously said, "Bisexuality immedi-ately doubles your chances for a date on Saturday night." As a bisexual woman, I can attest that this is not necessarily true. Bisexuality is more than just a math equation and cannot be so easily categorized or summarized. Identifying as bi, or being attracted to or engaging in sex with a variety of genders is the theme of this anthology, and indeed the term is much broader than just that dual opportunity. This is not a book about choosing either/or, male or female, or simply one of each. It's not about narrowing gender down to one size fits all, but about expanding our options, to a both/and approach to how we view and cultivate our sexuality. It's a welcoming, inclusive definition that welcomes all comers—pun fully intended.

I wanted this book, while fictional and focused on the erotic aspects of bisexual women's lives, to explore as wide a swatch of "bisexual" as possible. That means that some of the best stories here don't mention the word *bisexual* at all; they don't have to, because their bi angle, their queerness, is embedded—

and bedded—in the story. The characters are living it, rather than identifying with it; the sexual exploration and attraction, the experience and movement, are more important than what anyone wants to call it.

The large majority of the submissions I received for this book were about women having sex with women, which makes sense in the context of a culture that still privileges heterosexual identity over any other kind. Even in an era of so-called lesbian and bisexual chic, there's still plenty of discomfort with the fluidity with which many women view their sexuality. Shifting away from a purely heterosexual mindset forces women to grapple with the ways we differ from mainstream society, even one that is becoming much more open and knowledgeable about the varieties of queer life. The first time we dare to dip our toes—or other body parts—into the world of sex with other women is often momentous. Many of us will find the character of Laura, in Nicole Wolfe's opening story, "1 Percent Adaptable," familiar. Laura at first protests Marie's advances, warning her that she's not gay, not bi, until she listens to her body and follows its yearnings. "Laura was shocked that the kiss had surprised her, considering what had just happened between her legs. She let her lips caress Marie's. She dared to let her tongue out to play. She risked letting her hands tickle Marie's hips and backside," Wolfe writes.

But I didn't want this to simply be a first-time bi-curious tentative collection, but a robust one exploring the intimacy of life as a woman interested in men and women. That's why I wanted stories that asked questions like the ones in Jacqueline Applebee's closing tale, "What I Want, What I Need": "I'd been out as a lesbian since I was twenty-three. Why was I suddenly spending time with a straight man? Why was I enjoying it so much? Had I really been a lesbian at all, or had I been lying to myself for the past twenty years?"

There are girlfriends and wives, husbands and boyfriends, first dates, threesomes and much more here. There's daring and adventure, women taking risks by stepping outside their comfort zones, whether it's by surrendering to a bodyguard in "The State," by Tahira Iqbal, or confronting "The Wife" of a male lover in Kay Jaybee's story, only to be confronted right back. The women you'll read about are attracted to strong women like "The Robber Girl" in Lori Selke's story, and men who surprise them with their sensitivity, as in my story, "A Little Fun."

There's also kink, if that's what you're looking for. In Cheryl B.'s "The Break," spanking becomes a way for two exes to reconnect and revive the passion between them, while Sinclair Sexsmith takes us inside a gay bar and then home with a boy her protagonist has met there, one who may or may not know her true gender, in "Right-Red Flagging." The protagonist of "Seduction Dance," D, is under the watchful eye of her master when she finds a new female plaything for her to command and seduce. Gender is played with, fucked with, and grappled with as well in Giselle Renarde's "Glitter in the Gutter," in which the female partner of a male cross-dresser encourages his interest when he fears he's crossed a line and doesn't want to live in the new, judgmental world he's stepped into. Aimee Pearl writes in "Meeting at the Hole in the Wall," "Chivalry is dead, and I want to writhe naked on its grave."

These are celebratory, sexy stories, but, all apologies to Mr. Allen, they are more complex than a view of bisexuality simply as "twice as much" on offer. I like to think of them as both/ and stories that, collectively, offer a look at the ways bisexuality, queerness and lesbianism affect us while recognizing that there's no monolithic typical bisexual. We are multifaceted, full of desires that can't be contained in a single, simplistic category. We are hungry, horny, mischievous, naughty, provocative and, yes, curious. We may think we know what we want, only to keep on surprising ourselves just when we think we have it all figured out. We are open to a wide range of sexual possibilities, whether they exist in our heads or beyond.

I hope you'll enjoy the twenty-two stories presented here, and that they serve as erotic catalysts, no matter how you identify.

Rachel Kramer Bussel
New York City

1 PERCENT ADAPTABLE

Nicole Wolfe

You don't look like a health guru."

Laura turned from the luggage claim conveyor belt and looked down at the young Frenchwoman who had pronounced "guru" like it tickled her nose to say it.

"You are Laura Thacker, *oui?*"

"Yes," Laura said, with a bit more snap than she'd wanted. She was exhausted from the flight and wanted nothing more than a hot bath, a bar of dark chocolate, and silk sheets. "And you are?"

"Marie Kinnard. I am from Maintenant Books. Paul asked me to take care of you while you are in France."

Laura smiled. "Oh, of course." Her tensed shoulders dropped from being ready to box to a relaxed half-guard. Paul, her agent, had contacted each major bookstore chain she'd be visiting during the tour and asked them to provide an assistant to help her navigate the land, money, food and customs. So far they had all been bores, bitches or buffoons.

Marie, on the other hand, had an immediate calming effect. Her elegant features, crisp clothes and bobbed haircut almost made her look like either Louise Brooks or a *Blade Runner* replicant.

"I'm sorry if I snapped at you," Laura said. "The tour's been rough."

Marie put a delicate hand on her strong shoulder. "Oh, I am sorry. I hope I can make things better for you here in our country."

"As long as my luggage gets here, that'll be a start."

"I have your hotel room reserved, and our car is waiting."

Laura sighed in relief. If she had to catch one more bus or train or cab, she felt she'd break down in tears. Her bags flopped onto the conveyor belt. One of them, the one holding her workout gear, now sported a broken handle and a large rip across the top.

"Son of a bitch." Laura wanted to yell it, but she couldn't muster the strength.

"I will get you a new bag," Marie said, as she tried to lift it from the conveyor belt. The weight brought her motion to an abrupt halt and she almost fell to the floor. Laura rowed it off the belt with one hand.

"I packed way too much stuff for this trip," Laura said. "It's just so hard to get protein powder here in Europe."

Marie grabbed two of Laura's small bags from the belt. "You need it for your muscles, is that so? That is why I was surprised to see you."

"Yes. Is that what you meant about me not looking like a health guru?"

"*Oui.* I was told you were a best-selling fitness writer, but I expected someone else." She looked over Laura's solid shoulders and chiseled arms. "Someone not as strong."

Laura laughed for the first time in days. "You expected a skinny tofu eater, right? Not some big-boobed redhead."

Marie blushed. "I did. But you are a delightful surprise. You are very strong and..." She looked at Laura again, and there was a subtle change in her gaze that made Laura shift her weight back and forth a bit. "Very healthy. Yes. You are very healthy."

Laura slept during the limousine ride from the airport to the hotel. When she awoke, she discovered a silent movie seductress across from her sipping spring water and watching her come out of slumber.

"I'm in Paris, right?" Laura asked.

Marie laughed. "*Oui.*"

"I've been bounced around so much that I wouldn't be surprised if I were in China by now."

"Would you like dinner? The hotel has a wonderful restaurant."

"I could eat the ass end of a horse."

Marie's eyebrows went up. "*Quoi?*"

Laura smiled. "Sorry. I'm really hungry, yes."

Marie had Laura's bags sent up to her room and showed her to the restaurant. Laura was happier the moment she walked in and smelled the fresh bread. The place was upscale, but not so elegant that she'd need to choose between six different brands of water or be served nothing but an amazingly decorated asparagus spear.

"You said it has been a rough trip," Marie said as they started on their tomato bisque. "What has happened?"

"What hasn't happened? The tour's been rough from the start. Instead of starting in London, which would've been smart, my publisher scheduled the tour to start in Athens. I'm a sucker for Greek yogurt so I helped myself to the stuff my assistant stocked in my hotel fridge. I didn't notice it was expired so I had food poisoning in Athens for two days and missed most of my book signing there. Rome had better food but the hotel was a dump. The bed felt like the mattress was made of wet plywood and the air-conditioning didn't work. When the asshole cabbie dropped me off in the rain outside the bookstore he took off and soaked me head to toe. A drunk spilled a drink on me during the flight to Madrid. I had to catch a packed, sweaty bus from the airport and some guy was grabbing my ass the whole way."

Marie curled up her nose and made a small *tsk* sound.

"Oh, it gets worse," Laura said. "The Madrid hotel was the opposite of Rome. It had a nice bed but it was freezing cold all the time. I bitched about it, but it was never fixed. Their treadmill was fucked up so I tweaked my knee using it and the assistant there forgot to take me back to the airport, so I had to lug all my shit onto a train to get there and everyone at the airport had their prick meter on high."

Laura realized she was squeezing her butter knife like she was ready to yank open a shower curtain at the Bates Motel. She'd barely touched her bisque and salad. She was sweating. Her forehead was sore.

Marie tilted forward a bit. "You should eat. Good food will make you happy."

"You're probably right," Laura said and pulled off a hunk of baguette. She bit into it and sighed at its warmth. She could've stuffed her belly with it, but she reminded herself to watch her carbs. The bisque was heavenly. The salad was so good that she almost forgot to finish the bisque. She had it and the salad done and was ready to attack the baguette again when the coq au vin arrived. The smell made her moan. The taste made her speechless.

Cocktails were brought. Marie questioned the waiter, who pointed at two women at the bar. They were well dressed, naturally beautiful, and seated so close to each other that their knees were intertwined.

Laura had been in gyms a long time. She knew the signs. "Did those two just buy us drinks?"

Marie smiled. "*Oui*. They told the waiter they want us to have a good evening."

"They think we're another couple?" Laura blushed. She toasted the women, who smiled and returned a toast that included an unspoken invitation to join them. Laura looked back to her coq au vin before she made a fool of herself.

"That was nice of them," Laura said, "but I hope they don't think I'm rude by not joining them."

"You are very fit," Marie said. "They find you as attractive as a man would."

"Hell, maybe I should try my luck."

Marie's cocktail glass stopped short of her lips. "You should?"

Laura laughed. "No. I love men too much. I mean, I suppose if I had enough of these," Laura held up her cocktail, "I might be one percent adaptable."

Marie laughed now. "Perhaps they will send you more."

"Well, I haven't had much luck with men lately."

"Really?"

"It's half the reason I went on this book tour. My husband and I are separated. He said he wanted space. I think I'd be less pissed if he just said he wanted a divorce instead of this vague bullshit. I think he's fucking this waitress at the coffee shop around the corner from our house. He's supposed to be moved out by the time I get back."

"It is good he is leaving," Marie said. "It means he will have to crawl back to you."

They clinked glasses. "Amen, sister," Laura said.

After dinner and extra drinks, Marie showed Laura to her room. Laura smiled at seeing the luxurious king-sized bed, bowl of fresh fruit, vase of beautiful flowers and massive bathtub.

"I hope it suits you," Marie said.

"It's great," Laura said. "I'll sleep like a rock."

Marie turned for the door. "I will leave you to it. I will pick you up tomorrow at ten." She opened the door but stopped in her tracks as Laura made a sad moan from the bedroom.

Marie peeked around the corner. "Laura? Is something wrong?"

Laura stood next to a small table. One of her suitcases sat open on it and the inside was splattered with shampoo, lotion and sunscreen. Tears trickled down Laura's face as she stared into the bag.

"They didn't put my stuff back in the Ziploc bags at customs. It's everywhere."

"I will take care of it," Marie said.

"How? I don't have anything to wear."

"Right now," Marie said as she took Laura's hand and kissed her palm, "that does not matter."

Laura froze. "What are you doing?"

Marie kissed her pulsing wrist and then the inside of her elbow. "Why do you think those women thought we were a couple?"

Laura hadn't moved. "You... You're..."

Marie pressed against Laura and kissed her rock-solid shoulder. "Of course."

"But Marie, I'm not—"

"But you have not moved," Marie said. She gave Laura a peck on the throat and massaged her flat stomach.

Laura hadn't moved. She couldn't. Marie's delicate hand caressed her breasts through her shirt and her little mouth left

little lipstick prints across her collarbone. Laura felt an over-
powering urge to run, then another to relax and then another
to pick up this exotic woman and press her against the nearest
wall while they kissed.

But Marie wouldn't have that. She pushed Laura's shirt up as
she whispered little French dirty words to her. She licked a hot
line along the bottom of Laura's bra. Laura's bra soon fell to the
floor and she was shocked to realize she'd taken it off herself.

Marie cooed in delight and began licking small circles all
over Laura's tits. Laura trembled. She didn't know where this
was going to end, if she wanted it to end or how it even all
began. All she knew was that this woman she could easily bench
press had complete control of her.

Marie's mouth found one of Laura's nipples. Laura gasped
and her hands jumped up to grab Marie by the shoulders. She
did not pull her away. Her hands relaxed and started to massage
Marie's back. Marie nuzzled between Laura's tits and kept
speaking in a muffled dirty French that was a hypnotizing chant
to Laura's brain.

Marie got Laura's pants open. Laura didn't resist. Marie
pushed them to the floor and Laura stepped back to free herself
from them. Marie, who'd had so much trouble with a piece of
heavy luggage, pushed Laura back toward the bed with one
fingertip on Laura's quivering stomach.

Laura found her voice once the backs of her legs touched the
side of the bed. "Marie, I don't know—"

Marie put her finger over Laura's lips. Laura's tongue darted
out to taste it but jumped back into her mouth just as quick.
Marie's fingertips pushed Laura down to the bed by her shoulders. Laura arched her hips for her and let her pull her thong
down and off. Marie's hands slid up, up, and up. She pushed
Laura's goose-pimpled thighs apart until her thumbs stroked

over her lips and coaxed more wetness from her.

Laura jumped as Marie's thumbs brushed her clit. She clenched the sheets and felt her pussy pulling in Marie's fingers. Her breath quickened and she clamped her eyes shut, trying not to think about it. She didn't want to admit it. She thought if she held back, maybe Marie would realize...

Marie did realize exactly what was happening. Laura knew it. Laura knew Marie had felt how wet and hot she'd become since the first kiss on her hand. Laura knew that Marie had her close. She knew Marie was aware of how much she was enjoying this and how much she needed this.

Her tiny tongue. Such a small thing, but so warm and strong and practiced. Her tiny tongue on Laura's hard clit while her three fingers fucked her. Her hot mouth clamped on her now and a flood of come unleashed down her throat. Laura let loose with a cry that could be heard down the hall. She clamped on to Marie's head with one hand and bucked her pussy on her little pretty face. She held nothing back. She had been building this orgasm for over a week but hadn't known it. She gave it all to Marie, who never stopped licking and fucking her.

A warm fog had filled the hotel room. As it cleared from Laura's vision she saw and felt Marie, now naked, crawling up her body. Her porcelain skin, perky tits and bald snatch all looked delectable. Laura didn't know where to begin. Marie rubbed her wet, hot cunt on Laura's thigh for a few moments while she whispered more French dirty talk.

She bent down and kissed Laura full on the mouth for the first time. Laura was shocked that the kiss had surprised her, considering what had just happened between her legs. She let her lips caress Marie's. She dared to let her tongue out to play. She risked letting her hands tickle Marie's hips and backside.

Marie smiled and moved one of Laura's hands around to her

pussy. Laura gasped at the feel of it. She marveled at how tight Marie was and how her wet muscles clamped on to her and helped Laura fuck her. Marie rocked on Laura's hand while she held tiny handfuls of Laura's tits to keep from falling forward.

Laura knew enough to do what she liked doing to herself. She slid her fingers back and forth from Marie's pussy to her clit. She sank two fingers in, slid them out, rubbed Marie's clit; slid her fingers back in, back out, and kept it up until Marie's fingernails sank into her shoulders. Her head snapped back and she yelled at the ceiling. She soaked Laura's hand and then collapsed atop her. She trembled like someone had just thrown a bucket of cold water on her.

Laura wasn't sure when they fell asleep, but Marie was gone when she awoke. The room still smelled of their musk, so Laura knew she hadn't slept long. She found a note left on a pillow near her head.

I drew you a bath.

Laura smiled. It was exactly what she needed. She was still horny and a hot bath would be a nice cap to what had turned out to be a great evening.

She squeaked in surprise as she opened the bathroom door.

Marie sat in the bathtub that was big enough for three. Soap-suds stopped just above her nipples and she held two glasses of champagne. A tray of fresh fruit and cheese was on the floor next to the tub.

"You did draw me a bath," Laura said.

"I did. I thought you needed it." Marie's smile changed from sweet to naughty. "Do you need it, Laura?"

Laura stepped into the tub.

THE WIFE

Kay Jaybee

Jade walked slowly along the right-hand corridor, wiping her clammy palms self-consciously down the front of her jeans. Barely noticing the hospital's sterile cream walls that were hung with the occasional bizarrely abstract painting designed to cheer an otherwise depressing atmosphere, she turned left, left again, and then right, until she saw the small reception desk she'd been hunting for.

There were two women behind the desk, each with a computer terminal flashing before them, their fingers dancing over the attached keyboards. The identity tags they wore around their necks hung on long straps that reached below the line of the desk, so Jade was unable to see which of the women was the one she was hunting for.

"Can I help you?"

Jade had been expecting the question, but it still made her flinch as she was regarded by the pale-blue eyes of a pretty blonde woman, with a young, kind smile. "I, um…I'm searching for Karen Marks."

The other receptionist looked up, a questioning expression crossing her oval face. "That's me."

She had a darker complexion than Jade had imagined. Long black hair hung loose down her back, her eyes shone green and her skin glowed with the remnants of a tan. Jade suddenly realized she shouldn't have been surprised by that; after all, she already knew this woman had been to Spain within the last month.

Feeling her mouth go dry, Jade was unable to speak in the face of the striking thirtysomething woman before her. Karen Marks was far more attractive than she had allowed herself to imagine. There was something disconcerting about the mistress discovering that the wife was an eye-catching, self-assured woman, and not the cold harridan who had been portrayed to her. No, that wasn't true. Neil had never told her what Karen looked like, or even what she was like. Jade had never asked him. She had simply presumed. She had presumed wrong.

"I..." Jade licked her lips nervously. "I wonder if we could have a quick word in private."

Karen's eyes narrowed and the curt nod of her head told Jade that somehow she'd been expecting her visit, if not today, then one day. Addressing her colleague, she said, "I might as well take my lunch now," and rose from her chair before leaving the office. "This way." Jade had to jog to keep up as Karen's long, slender legs marched down a neighboring corridor, her heels clicking purposefully against the tiled floor, before she disappeared into a side room.

The small space had once been a treatment room, but now it was storage for unused medical equipment. Boxes were haphazardly piled up and scattered around an old ripped examination couch.

When she finally turned to face Jade, Karen's expression was strangely calm. "So, how long?"

"Six months."

"And why come to me now?"

Jade could barely hear her own answers, such was the hammering of the blood in her ears as she faced her lover's wife. Mustering all her concentration on keeping her voice level, she replied, "One of Neil's colleagues found out. He threatened to tell you. I didn't want you to find out like that."

Karen propped herself against the examination bed, holding her arms protectively across her chest. "You thought this less cruel?"

Jade nodded shyly. "It seemed like the responsible thing to do."

"Responsible?" Karen spoke the word with incredulity. She cocked her head to one side, an expression of disbelief on her face, rather than the angry or distraught one Jade had been mentally preparing herself for. "What does Neil think about this? He does know you're here, right?"

"Well, actually he thought it was a mad idea, but yes, he knows I'm here."

"Let me guess—he told you he didn't want you to come?" Karen sat farther back on the torn couch and crossed her long legs, showing Jade how shapely they were beneath her black work trousers, making her wonder why on earth Neil had sought out her much shorter, more rounded frame. His wife certainly didn't appear to be the type of woman who'd be lacking in the sex department.

Jade bent her head away from the increasingly uncomfortable stare of her opponent. Karen's sharp eyes didn't even seem to blink. This wasn't how Jade had imagined this confrontation at all. She'd prepared herself for anger, tears, accusations and perhaps even physical violence, but not mild disdain, and certainly not derisive amusement. As the quiet piercing gaze continued, Jade felt a steeling unease creep up her spine. "I should go; I thought you should know from one of us, not from some third party. That's all."

Karen snorted. "Third party! Isn't that what you are, honey?" Her words cut like ice, her lips barely moving as she spat them out. "Wouldn't you say that this colleague was, in fact, the fourth party?"

"I suppose." Mumbling her words, Jade hoisted her handbag up onto her shoulder; she'd been gripping it so tightly that the leather strap had begun to dig into her palm.

"Tell me," Karen recrossed her arms, crushing her tits under her creamy satin blouse, so that her cleavage was pushed up even higher, "what makes you so sure that this *colleague* actually exists?"

"What?" Jade frowned.

"Couldn't Nick be bored with you, like he got bored with all the others before you?"

A cold wave of panic swept through Jade as Karen jumped from the couch, standing so near that Jade could feel her warm breath against her face. Trying to avoid the wife's glare, but also determined not to look at her undeniably gorgeous chest, Neil's mistress kept her eyes fixed on her feet, and attempted to step away from the receptionist. However, Jade was hemmed in and had no choice but to hold her ground. Confusion swamped her.

"You did know he'd done this before?" Karen tilted her head to one side, appraising her visitor. "No, I can see he has told you nothing of the other gullible women who have come to find me like this."

"What...I..." The words "gullible" and "women" stuck in Jade's ears, echoing over and over again.

Jade stepped sideways in an attempt to put some distance between herself and her lover's wife, but Karen's arm shot out, her hand catching Jade expertly around the wrist. Its cool, tight grip pinched. "We are not done here yet, honey." She gestured to the couch with her head, her sleek hair swaying with the abrupt movement. "Sit."

Her feet stayed where they were. The small hairs at the back of Jade's neck prickled as her mind raced.

"I told you to sit." Karen propelled the smaller woman by the elbow to the couch. "I advise you to do as you are told. After all, I think you'd agree that you and Neil owe me one—or probably more than one if I know Neil, which my dear girl, I do. Very well indeed." Karen closed the door of the room and pushed a few boxes in front of it, ensuring they would not be disturbed.

Jade's heart rate went off the scale as an unfamiliar combination of fear, panic and intense curiosity filled her. She knew she should run, scream, call for help, but something about this woman made her stay precisely where she was. A vision of Neil flashed through her head. Had he set her up to come here with tales of a fictitious colleague? Was he just trying to get rid of her, or, perhaps his wife had orchestrated this, perhaps it was her...

The hand around her bare arm relaxed its grip a little, but Karen didn't let go. Instead, she began to trail her neatly trimmed, black-painted fingernails up and down a square inch of Jade's skin, sending electric waves of unexpected desire through Jade's body. "So, let me look at you properly; let me see exactly what my husband sees in a little girl like you."

Jade trembled beneath the woman's oppressive gaze. She felt as though she was being appraised before being sent to market. The slim-fit jeans and respectable short-sleeved lilac shirt she had believed suitably dowdy for the occasion felt not only slutty but see-through. She longed to flick a stray red hair from her eyes, but any movement she might make could be wrong, forbidden—or worse, misinterpreted as encouragement.

The green eyes after which she had been named felt dim next to the catlike sheen of Karen's stare, which started at Jade's small booted feet and traveled up the length of her five-foot-two pale frame, making Jade embarrassingly conscious of her hardening nipples. This was ridiculous. Although the thought wasn't unappealing, she certainly didn't really want to have her first experience of sleeping with a woman with an intimidating wronged wife, especially when she was the one who'd wronged her. *Why the hell is my body responding in this way? What is the matter with me?* "Let me go!"

"I don't think so, honey." Karen's tongue dripped scorn. "You owe me one fuck at least." Karen ran a sensual digit across Jade's chest. "And by the way, your tits are reacting to me, my dear. I'd say you quite like the idea."

Jade froze as Karen's palms pressed against her breasts, forcing her to shuffle backward, so she was flat against the wall. Her feet felt glued to the floor as her treacherous tits pushed hungrily back at the uninvited pressure.

Karen came closer, dropping her hands to Jade's waist, her own rounded chest brushing her opponent's. She whispered into Jade's ear, "Neil tells me everything, you know. Everything..."

Flinching as the other woman's mouth came to her neck, Jade let out a muffled cry as her skin was nipped and lapped with long, languid strokes. Unable to move, and with no choice but to endure the attention, Jade screwed up her eyes and tried to focus on Neil. He hadn't really told his wife about her...had he? Had there really been others? Surely Karen was just trying to freak her out, trying to extract her revenge in the strangest way possible.

When the red lipstick-covered lips met hers, Jade was totally unprepared for the current of electricity that shot from her mouth to between her legs, and was unable to hide the quiet groan that revealed her body wanted this, even if her brain screamed that she didn't.

Laughing, Karen said, "I knew it; you're like a bitch in heat." She pulled the shirt from Jade's trousers and thrust her hands beneath then, scratching sharp nails across Jade's flat stomach. "I bet if I touched your pussy it would drip between my fingers."

Squirming, Jade tried to pull away, but was again prevented by Karen, the wall behind her and the boxes that littered the floor. "I don't want this. You're crazy!"

Karen's hand moved so fast Jade didn't have time to prepare for the arrival of the slap that stung her cheek. "Crazy? I don't think so. Just curious, girlie, curious about who is currently getting my husband's boxers around his ankles on a Tuesday afternoon."

Jade's throat instantly dried shut, as she croaked out a bewildered, "Tuesdays? How did you know that we met on Tuesdays?"

Karen laughed again, this time with less cruelty and more pity, which seemed somehow worse to Jade, as the woman stroked her lithe body. "I told you, little girl, Neil tells me *everything*." She worked her hands up under her rival's bra, pinching her nipples until tears sprung up in Jade's eyes. "Haven't you worked it out yet?"

"I..." Jade couldn't think what else to say. Her arms hung limply at her sides as a hot, tight pain coursed through her chest, and her brain tangled with conflicting messages, telling her to both run and hide, and stay and enjoy these strange new sensations as the warm body caressed her own.

"Let me tell you a few facts." Karen's eyes blazed as she spoke, her fingers continuing to work Jade's nipples. "One: Neil and I have an arrangement regarding third parties to our marriage.

Two: Neil only goes for women he thinks I will find attractive—until now, that is. You really are something completely different from his usual type, hence my curiosity. Three: he has been on a search, a quest, if you like. A search I sent him on... I can't believe he found *you*, though," she sneered in derision. "Still, I suppose he *might* be right. I find you something of a puzzle, little girl. You're fighting what I'm doing, yet you aren't trying to push me away. You are deliciously aroused, in spite of your natural personal feelings of wariness toward me." Karen squeezed Jade's tips even harder, making her sob gasps of pain, unable to believe what she was hearing, unable to comprehend that her body was responding so much to the other woman, while her sticky liquid glued her satin knickers to her crotch as Karen continued. "Usually Neil's conquests either break away from me and run away, never to be seen by either Neil or me again, or they willingly enjoy a quick tumble and leave. You, my dear, are different."

Ripping the zip-fly of Jade's jeans open, Karen thrust an arm into the gap and grabbed Jade's pussy through her panties, making her squeal in a heady mix of protest and dark pleasure. "I knew it!" The wife's voice was triumphant. "They're wet! You are one hot handful."

Jade said nothing, biting back tears of humiliation. Two conflicting voices shouted at the back of her head, one asking her why she hadn't run away, the other telling her to relax and savor the new experience.

"Now come with me." Dragging Jade by the crotch to the battered medical couch, Karen pulled down her jeans, saying, "Sit."

Jade found herself sitting, her body working as if on autopilot. She reclosed her eyes, feeling heavy, weak, confused and helpless to do anything but obey, as her companion began to massage her cunt through the fabric of her damp knickers. Karen, commanding but calm, used her free hand to open the buttons of Jade's shirt, revealing the small neat globes with her bra hanging uselessly above them. "That's a good girl. Now, you stay precisely where you are."

The stale, cool air of the medical junk room blew around them, feeling unbelievably arousing against Jade's skin as Karen slid her pants down. Working skilled fingers over the sticky nub, Karen released a deep breath, a smirk of triumphant command across her face, as she dug a hand into her pocket and pulled out a mobile phone.

Jade snapped her eyes open as she heard talking. "I have her here." Clutching her husband's lover's snatch even harder, the expression on Karen's face dared her victim to speak as she chatted in relaxed tones. "She's much younger and smaller than your usual type, darling."

Her face blanched as Jade realized that everything Karen had said was true. Neil had been in on this from the start. He had known *exactly* what would happen when she came here today. She was about to speak, when Karen eased a long index finger into Jade's wet opening, changing her forthcoming words of protest into an unbidden sigh of lust.

"But you were right, babe, she is one horny bitch." Karen chuckled at Neil's unheard reply. "She's done nothing but complain since she got here, but boy, is she hot. You should see her right now, her clothes are in disarray, and she's skewered on my finger, moaning like a common whore."

Karen beamed into the receiver, and Jade could only guess what her lover was saying to his wife, flushing in shame as she accepted the truth of the situation.

Yet the idea of Neil being high on the knowledge of her current situation was strangely erotic, as was the power of the woman whose finger was now sliding in and out of her with painfully slow regularity. Beneath the dark of her eyelids, Jade could picture Neil, his trousers around his ankles, his boxers down, a firm hand around his hard shaft, yanking himself off as his wife described exactly what she was doing to his lover.

It was a thought too far—the images in Jade's head, the tightness of her breasts, and the finger that was probing up inside her were all pushing her body farther toward the edge. Shutting her eyes tighter so as not to witness even a glimpse of the inevitable expression of victory on her companion's face, Jade allowed her body to receive the climax it so desperately needed.

"Oh, sweetheart!" Karen's gloat down the phone only made Jade feel smaller than ever. "I hardly touched her, and she's fucked off against my hand."

There was a pause as Neil obviously spoke to his wife at length. Jade, her eyes still fused, hardly dared breathe, her ears straining to hear what he was saying. After a few moments of fruitless listening, she heard Karen say, "Okay, darling, will do," before she ended the call.

"Well, then." Karen drew her hand free, making Jade whimper at its loss and her companion laugh as she sucked Jade's juices from her hand. "You have just managed to make your master come. I hope you're proud." Jade said nothing. She had never thought of Neil in terms of being her master before. It was another disconcerting thought to add to all the others that were swimming around her head. "You are obviously a powerful force in my husband's imagination."

Suddenly Jade realized that she wasn't being touched or restrained any more, and gradually she opened her eyes. Karen stood before the couch gazing directly at her. Her blouse was open, and one hand was twisting her right nipple, while the other was down her trousers. From the look on her face, she was fast bringing herself off. Jade couldn't help but wordlessly watch. She had never witnessed a woman wanking before, and felt her enflamed and confused body begin to respond as she observed the scene in fascination.

A sharp cry and Karen, her eyes locked onto Jade's, indicated the start of a juddering climax that left her shaking for only the briefest of moments. Then, in a brisk, businesslike way, she did up her clothes, brushed herself off, and, with cold indifference, as if nothing had happened, said, "For god's sake, woman, have some pride, will you? Get dressed, I've got work to do."

Shakily, Jade got to her feet and readjusted her clothing. Picking up her bag, she stood up. She wanted to run as far away from this strange woman as possible, but at the same time Jade desperately needed to know what Neil had said to his wife on the phone. She had only taken two steps toward the door before she decided that as her pride and dignity had already been torn to shreds, she might as well ask. *What have I got to lose now anyway?* "What did he say on the phone?"

Karen smiled insincerely. "Ask him yourself, little girl. He's coming to see you tonight." Then Mrs. Marks pushed roughly past her husband's mistress before adding, without so much as a backward glance, "And I'm coming, too..."

OPERETTA

Jean Roberta

Why did I do it? Because he asked for it, that's why.

Luke was an unpublished poet (waiter by night) with a strong nose and glossy dark-brown hair that fell adorably into his eyes. When he asked me to write one of my sex fantasies, how could I resist? We had been talking about forbidden teenage lust, and had told each other about the books we used to read by flashlight under the covers when our parents thought we were asleep.

I gave him a reading list of classic scandalous novels and sex manuals, and we agreed to discuss each one after he finished reading it.

The next time he came over, I was prepared. He patted his lap and I sat there, my bare asscheeks pressed against his rising cock, a clear indicator of his mood. The musk from his armpits rose to my nose like incense. I had one arm around his hard, smooth shoulders to keep my balance while I reached for a sheaf of typed pages with the other.

I knew that Luke enjoyed the touch of my hardening nipples

against his hairy chest. My breasts are a modest size but they are perky, and he seemed to admire them, judging from the amount of attention he always gave them. It was part of his charm.

I read him the stage directions of my fantasy:

"Enter the Author in raven ringlets, a scarlet petticoat and white satin corset with a few laces undone. She carries a basket of red berries that she occasionally holds to her chest while she pulls a rosy nipple out of her décolletage. She is Modest Maggie of the Market."

I gathered my breath, and tried to sing quietly. After all, my voice didn't have to fill an auditorium.

"I am the very model of a willing pleasure-giver-er.

I'll do things to your ticklish parts to make them swell and quiver-er.

You've never seen my like before.

I'll always leave you wanting more.

I am the very model of a practiced pleasure giver-er."

Luke shifted under me and let out a sound that could have been a quiet chuckle or just a loud exhale. "That's different."

"It's based on Gilbert and Sullivan," I explained. "You know, the two guys who wrote a whole series of comic operettas in the late nineteenth century. The time of Queen Victoria. My parents had a set of records, and my mom used to play them while she did the housework. The Light Opera Society puts on one every year."

Luke seemed bewildered. "Classical music, eh? It's good you learned all about that stuff when you were growing up, but now you're your own woman, honey. I know you can write some hot sex stories."

I felt as if he had slapped me, and not in a good way. "This is a sex story, Luke. It's the kind of raunchy musical I wish Gilbert and Sullivan had written. It's what I imagined when

I listened to their patter songs on the stereo. The situation has to be presented, then there has to be a buildup of tension, then everyone gets together in an orgy on a pirate ship. I'd like to stage it for the right audience."

I could feel that Luke's cock was not convinced. Luke himself liked to say he was open-minded. "Okay. Go on."

I read more stage directions:

"A crowd of other peddlers, gentlemen customers and other urban street-types, including disapproving Salvation Army ladies in black bonnets, surround Maggie."

I sang with more exuberance than before, trying to impersonate a general chorus:

"She is the very model of a practised pleasure-giver-er!"

Luke looked thoughtful, and stroked one of my thighs. I hoped this was a good sign, so I soldiered on with more stage directions:

"A constable strides past, looking round suspiciously and fondling his truncheon, but he doesn't arrest Maggie because her true profession is a secret. A crew of colorfully dressed pirates rushes onstage. One plays a whistle while the others dance a hornpipe."

"What's a hornpipe?" Luke sounded like a polite high school student.

"A dance that British sailors always do in nineteenth-century novels and plays," I explained. "You know." I hummed a melody into Luke's nearest ear so he could feel the vibrations. He laughed.

I went on. "Then the Pirate Captain says, *You're coming with us, wench. We need a pleasure-giver on our ship full of booty.*" I said this line in the deepest growl I could pull up from my depths. I tried to speak in the voice of my cunt.

Luke tightened his grip on me, and his own truncheon made

itself felt. "So the pirates all screw her?"

"Something like that. But it's complicated because there's a woman pirate who wants her, too, and the forces of law and order want to stop all this from happening."

"Yeah, I guess they would," said Luke philosophically. "Back in those days."

Before he could ask me to stop reading, I read more stage directions: "*The shortest pirate, with prominent breasts beneath her tight velvet jacket and lace jabot, elbows the others aside. She is Pirate Patty.*" Then I tried to channel the husky voice of a hearty butch: "*Step aside, lads. I'll take care of her.*"

"So is this a lesbian play? Do you just ditch all the men and do it with a chick in this piece?"

Why didn't I foresee that Luke would react this way? "No, Luke. You know I'm bi. I think I was bi even when I was in high school, but I didn't have a word for it then. I used to fantasize about female outlaws all the time, but it doesn't mean I wanted to give up guys for the rest of my life."

"I hope not." He still sounded uncomfortable.

"Pirate Patty explains herself in a song," I explained. I tried to sing in her voice:
"The flowers that bloom in the spring, tra la,
Have nothing to do with my life.
To men's arms I never would cling, tra la,
And I never will be a man's wife."

Then I took a deep breath and tried to channel the whole Pirate Chorus: "*Arrgh! She never will be a man's wife!*"

Luke turned me to face him. His eyes sparkled, and he looked amused. "A real male-basher even in the old days. I bet all the pirates tune her up."

Against my will, my mind's-eye flashed on a real-life scene of wartime chaos from the TV news: armed men hauling villagers, mostly women, out of their huts. The scene I refused to imagine was about women as the spoils of war, and not in a good way. I was getting turned off.

"Why, do you think all women should be married to men?" *Please, Luke,* I thought, *please don't say something stupid.*

Luke gently took the sheaf of paper from my hand and set it on the coffee table. "I never said that, honey. You know how I feel about marriage. I just don't think it's good for you to write men off altogether, you know? Just because I don't know all the things that are important to you and I'm not politically correct all the time, it doesn't mean I'm a total jerk. What kind of sex scene can you have if all the men are left holding their own meat while the girls, women, whatever, sail off to their own island?"

"You didn't let me finish," I sighed.

"I can write the climax," he grinned. Both his arms and his cock seemed to have hardened in seconds. "I think the Pirate Captain should carry Maggie the Slut to his cabin and show her a real good time."

I knew I couldn't get anywhere by talking to him about plot arcs and the kind of dramatic conventions that might even work in an X-rated operetta. My clit felt like a sulky child who resents being pulled away from a favorite game to eat ice cream. Ice cream is always welcome, but being interrupted is not.

Luke lowered his head to capture one of my nipples between his lips as though it were a ripe raspberry. He sucked it like a connoisseur, gradually increasing the pressure. His hot scalp gave off a scent of male sweat that appealed to me in spite of myself. Just when I thought Luke's sucking had stretched my nipple to its longest possible size, he flicked the tip with his tongue. I moaned.

Luke pulled away and licked his lips. "Arrgh," he said.

I laughed. Before I could catch my breath, Luke had fastened his hot, wet mouth on my other nipple to give it the same treatment.

He stroked my hair and wrapped some around one fist. For a man who didn't do much physical work, he had surprisingly large hands with hard skin and prominent knuckles. I couldn't help remembering the last time he had three fingers deep inside me.

I had balked at dyeing my brown hair blonde to please him, but I was willing to grow it, and it was now past shoulder-length. "Mm, wench." He used my hair to pull my head backward so I was looking up at him. "You get me going. You can't get out of it now."

I felt greedy, knowing that this relationship was speeding toward a dead end. I wanted him, for better or worse. I wanted something I could keep when his innocent male skin and muscles and smells and energy and simple beliefs were just a memory. "Oh, Captain," I cooed, "are you going to ravish me?"

"I'll fuck you till you're sore, girl. You have it coming." I wiggled against his rock-hard cock and felt it twitch. I almost regretted my unwillingness to take something that large in the small, puckered hole in my squeamish ass. I knew I had disappointed him when I turned down his suggestion. I had accepted anal plugs wielded by savvy women, but Luke's manly cock seemed less trustworthy. Of course, I reminded myself, its nature was part of its charm.

"Let's do it on the floor, Beth," he grunted.

I liked this idea because I wanted him in me as soon as possible. I couldn't be sure whether I was eager to come or eager to finish. "Oh, yes," I sighed.

He helped me to my feet and managed to lift me in his arms, grunting under his breath. He laid me on my back on the musty carpet that I hadn't vacuumed for a week. I gave him credit for not dropping me like a sack of potatoes. I wasn't heavy compared to other women, but I knew he wasn't used to carrying loads of my size.

He lowered himself over me, his hands on both sides of me like a cage. "Rrowr," he growled. I spread my legs, showing him my slit. I was sure the wetness had soaked my curly brown hair.

He kissed and licked his way down my ticklish midriff and sensitive tummy. When he reached my belly button, his tongue dipped in and made me giggle uncontrollably. As I squirmed beneath him, he reached down and held my hips in place. The heat and strength of his hands spread through my flesh until I felt as if my bones could melt.

He used two fingers to find my clit. He petted it lovingly, but he had another goal. He slipped one finger, then two fingers, into me, and they slid past my slippery folds until I felt them press against my cervix. His knuckles stroked all the right places as he explored my channel as though he wanted to learn every inch of it by heart. I felt little spasms like electric sparks in my core, and I knew I would come this time. I felt wet enough to leave a pool of my juice on the carpet.

Caveman, I thought, seeing the word in neon red against the soft darkness of my mind. I tried to erase it, and the letters faded gradually.

He rose up to reach the small, clear packet he had left on an end table, then used his teeth to open it. In a flash, his cock was sheathed and ready for action. He carefully held my lower lips apart while he guided his cock inside. It plunged in like a bolt sliding into the groove that was meant for it. "Beth," he groaned. No other words were necessary.

He filled me deliciously as he pumped in and out, galloping like a racehorse. I squeezed him with my cunt muscles as I held him with my arms, wanting the moment to last as long as possible. I could hear myself making sounds I could hardly recognize.

"Oh!" I sang out when the first real spasm hit me like lightning. I didn't need to fake it, and I was proud. So was Luke, and I felt his satisfaction as my clit erupted and my cunt clutched him over and over.

"Ahhh, here it comes," he bragged as he fucked without mercy, completely focused on his own pleasure now that I had crossed the finish line. His sweaty skin pressed against mine, and I cupped his hard buttcheeks in my small hands so I could feel his muscles working there.

He stroked my hair and face as his cock shrank and slipped out of me. "Beth." I could hear him breathe. "That was awesome."

I felt moved by his masculine grace, his appetite and his willingness to please. I could imagine him as a boy, and I wished I had known him then. He was not a bad sort, as one of my exes would have said.

I think we both knew that what he had to give me wasn't enough.

He moved first, and gave me enough room to get up off the floor and look for my clothes. His jeans and T-shirt were neatly folded on an arm of my sofa, and he shrugged them on without taking his eyes off me. My clothes were more scattered, and I dressed myself in stages: first the bra and panties, then the cotton pants, the sleeveless top, the cardigan, the socks. My hair kept falling in my eyes, so I looked for a scrunchie to hold it back. I felt as if I were changing roles.

He gave me a close, lingering hug and a generous good-bye kiss. "I have to go." He was stating the obvious to avoid stating the more obvious. "I'll call you, honey."

"I'll see you, Luke." I felt as fake as a ninety-pound woman with a pair of size 42DDs, but I didn't see how I could ask him not to call me, not to see me. I didn't want to end our relationship with an argument that neither of us could win.

He closed my door for the last time.

My sex fantasy seemed stupid to me, but I wanted to finish reading it from the viewpoint of someone like Luke. Not Luke himself, of course, because I already knew what he thought of it. I wanted to decide whether it had the genuine cheesiness of my youth.

I picked up where I had left off, reading to myself:

"Pirate Captain: But Maggie must be married to the shy First Mate! After she has pleasured all of us, of course.

Pirate Pete (a lanky red-faced man with a loud voice, clutching a bottle of rum): Arrgh! Share and share alike! That's the Pirate Code!

(A stout and resolute Salvation Army lady pushes her way past the pirates to the front of the stage. She is Captain Killjoy.)

CK: Maggie must be reformed and married to a respectable man with a good salary! This is a musical for families, and I am the voice of the Author's upbringing!

PP (with great sarcasm): Righto, sister. Take a stroll with me in the park, and we'll see who gets converted.

(First Mate Bashful Bert Bentley rushes nervously between LK and PP. His knees knock as he faces the audience.)

BBB: B-b-but I don't want to marry a woman! No disrespect intended, Maggie. Why d'youse think I signed on board a ship full of men! Excepting one, if you'll pardon me for saying so, Patty.

PP: No offense taken, Bert.

PC: Insubordination! Bert, you must be flogged. (To audience) He's such fun to flog.

LK: Flogging and prayer!

PP: Flogging and gamahouching! (To audience) That's oral sex to you. (Shocked, delighted gasp from the assembled company.) And dildoes! Nothing like them for enforcing pirate discipline! (A hushed moan passes through the company.)

MM: And for rewarding good service!

(Captain Killjoy faints and is dragged offstage. The constable pushes his way through the crowd. He is Officer Lance.)

OL: Here, you degenerates! The moral standards of our good Queen must triumph at last. Do the lot of you need a taste of my truncheon?

Pirate Chorus: Arrgh! Aye! Hip hip hooray!"

I hadn't written the orgy scene yet, and I suspected that I never would. I no longer had an audience.

Several days later, when I was grading student essays, I got an unexpected phone call. I really hadn't expected Andrew to phone me.

"Do you remember me?" he asked coyly. Duh. He had married my friend Jessie right out of high school, and they had driven each other crazy for five years. Officially, their divorce had been caused by her affair with her boss at work, but as soon as she and Andrew were living separately, he began frequenting a certain gay bar. He seemed to know all the waiters in town, including Luke. Andrew hadn't introduced us, but our shared connection with him had been the conversation-starter when Luke served me a cup of coffee while I was waiting for a woman who never showed up.

Andrew and I were connected by a dozen tangled threads.

"I've missed you, Beth. I liked having you around when I was with Jessie, but you know how that went." Andrew's voice was low and resonant, and it had a distinct rhythm. It sounded as if it should be coming from a man twice his size, and it attracted attention wherever he went.

I laughed. "I find you strangely appealing, too, Andrew. In our spare time, we could compare notes and produce a kind of *Michelin Guide* to local restaurant staff."

"You're a fountain of brilliant ideas, dear, but I'm calling about something else. I have a proposal for you." I suddenly imagined a comic wedding: Andrew and me, two short people in formal dress, marrying for some bizarre reason that would be revealed in another scene.

I waited.

"You know I'm directing Little Theater this season, don't you? I have a big role to fill, and I'm afraid I need someone yesterday. Would you like to try out for the lead in *Hedda Gabler*?"

"Me?" I didn't understand it. "Don't you know someone with more experience?" I stopped myself from reminding him that he probably knew some drag queens who could do a passable job in the role of that unhappy Nordic woman, a Valkyrie in the closet.

"You underestimate yourself, girl. But there is another role you could apply for. Have you ever sung in a slightly naughty musical?"

I sang: *"I am the very model of a willing pleasure-giver-er.*
I'll do things to your ticklish parts to make them swell and quiver-er.
You've never seen my like before.
I'll always leave you wanting more.
I am the very model of a practiced pleasure-giver-er."

In my own defense, I must admit that I had had a glass of wine or two to help me get over my breakup with Luke.

I don't know what Andrew had been doing before he dialed my number, but by my last line, he was humming along. "I love it, Beth! I would promote you to Major General any day."

"Oh, sure." I felt foolishly flattered.

"The show I have in mind is a revival of burlesque. We need writers as well as performers." Why hadn't I heard of this project? Probably because it was brainstormed by a group of gay men who hadn't told anyone outside their circle yet.

In short, Andrew offered to take me out for dinner the following day to discuss his plans and my availability. He appeared promptly at my door in a suit, his sandy-blond hair mussed and gelled to perfection.

Over Coquilles St-Jacques at Chez Pierre, he openly held my hand on the white linen tablecloth. I assumed that the candlelight was too dim to allow our waiter to see our fingers entwined, and thus we were spared a jealous hissy fit.

"I have another proposal, Beth." He gave me his most charming smile. "You know I'm bi, don't you?"

I nodded. "There's a lot of that going around."

"You know that Oscar Wilde and young Lord Alfred were called 'friends,' don't you? And that Radclyffe Hall had a 'friend' in society named Mabel before Una became her 'friend' to the end?"

"Would you like us to be 'friends,' Andrew?"

"I would be honored, Beth. I would have liked to stay friends with Jessie, but she couldn't deal with it. I think you could."

I smiled. "I think you're right."

Later, on Andrew's ridiculously high four-poster bed, surrounded by fat cushions, I let him pose me on all fours, sitting, lying on my side, facedown and faceup while he commented on my best angles. He lifted my hair and twisted it into various shapes. He was shamelessly visual. He showed me an impressive hard-on, and its redness contrasted with his pale thighs. "It's blushing," I told him.

"You could hide him," grinned Andrew, my friend with benefits. "Are you a sword-swallower, Beth?"

I had expected this question, and I'd brought my own supplies. As an answer, I dressed his hard cock in a clear protective covering, opened my mouth, relaxed my throat and sucked in the whole thing. I assumed he was a connoisseur of this act. He seemed overwhelmed by my performance, judging from his reaction.

As a reward or possibly from curiosity, Andrew spread my legs and studied my wet opening as though it were the entrance to an undiscovered continent. "I truly love this," he told me. "Every woman has her own bouquet."

He wanted to taste my naked flesh, and I didn't want to stop him. He sucked, licked and nibbled all the wetness he could reach, and I felt as if my clit and my cunt had been starved for attention before that night. He savored my taste until I thought I would explode, but I imploded instead, losing control and shattering inside while bright colors formed a kaleidoscope in my mind. While I lay in his comforting arms, I felt as if I could float.

"I hope you have the energy for a few more rounds before we sleep, dear." Andrew looked at me as if he had just told me a juicy secret and trusted me to keep it. "You're very versatile, aren't you?"

"I try." I loved his hardy compactness and his own ability to play different roles on different occasions.

"There's so much I'd love to do with you." He sounded lecherous.

"Please be patient, Andrew." I tried to look demure. "I'm willing to expand my repertoire."

He hummed a pretty melody under his breath, and I knew even before I recognized it that it must be a love-duet from a musical comedy.

LIFELINE

Emerald

C helsea scrubbed her fingers with a nail brush, trying to erase the inevitable grime of working at Carter's Auto Service. Yawning, she rinsed her hands, their cleanliness reaching the peak of where they were going to get, and returned to her bedroom.

She sat down at the vanity and uncapped the tiny bottle of nail glue. Carefully, she brushed her left thumb with the miniature applicator and picked up the first of ten artificial nails arranged on the glass in front of her. She pressed it into place, glancing at the clock as she held it for several seconds to let the glue dry.

When her nails were applied, all but obliterating any evidence of the grunge of her day job, Chelsea located her heels and dropped them in her bag. Rummaging through her wardrobe to find what she would wear that night, she pulled out a minuscule tube dress and stuffed it into the bag as well, threw her curling iron in on top of it and grabbed her purse on the way out the door.

The parking lot of the Silver Dollar, which didn't open for another half hour, was mostly empty as she pulled in. Chelsea parked near the entrance and grabbed her gear from the front seat. Making her way to the opaque door that had become familiar over the last three months, she pushed through it without pausing—thus making the transition from Chelsea to Mickey.

She saw Jocelyn right away. Chelsea's nerves began to tingle like vibrating cello strings as Jocelyn caught sight of her and headed her way with a smile.

"Mickey!" The warm greeting, filled with affection Chelsea knew was strictly friendly, made Chelsea's nerves vibrate harder nonetheless. Jocelyn wrapped her in a hug then let go to ask Chelsea how she was. Her dark eyes offered the undivided attention that made her one of the most consistently successful dancers at the club. Which happened, Chelsea knew, without Jocelyn's even trying. Jocelyn loved her job, for sure, but she also loved people, which was what Chelsea felt made people, including customers, love her so much back.

She, of course, loved Jocelyn more than most. As per usual, Chelsea squirmed internally at the intensity of the attraction and the knowledge that no one, with the exception of her friend Alex, knew about it, including the target of the infatuation herself.

It had been three months since Chelsea had started dancing at the Silver Dollar; three months since her mother had told her of her illness and Chelsea had been made aware that the forthcoming medical bills were going to be well beyond what her mother could afford. Chelsea remembered the first day she'd walked into the club and met Jocelyn's dark chocolate eyes— eyes that managed to make the goddess-like mocha body below them take second place, commanding all attention into their rich depths until they took it upon themselves to relinquish it.

On the stage, Jocelyn was almost beyond comprehension. With seamless elegance she would run her long nails up her smooth, dark skin, her black hair swirling into big curls at her shoulders. Her deep brown eyes missed no one as she ran them around the stage below her. When she smiled, usually looking from under her lashes in a pose rife with both coyness and allure, her teeth positively glimmered against the background of her magnificent ebony skin. She was beautiful.

Of course, most of her coworkers were beautiful. Even Chelsea herself had been told she was beautiful—here, anyway. It wasn't a compliment she recalled hearing much anywhere else.

But most of her coworkers weren't Jocelyn. Chelsea took a deep breath as she went to the dressing room to prepare for her set. She wondered as she brushed her blonde hair if it would be easier if she didn't see Jocelyn all the time—naked, no less. Much as she admired Jocelyn from afar, Chelsea had to endure interacting with her as a friend, too, the other woman's exquisite blend of innocence and awareness making her unbearably appealing while reducing Chelsea to what felt like a puddle of mindlessness.

Despite their friendship, Chelsea had no idea if Jocelyn was interested in women. Working up the nerve to approach someone she had a crush on had always been challenging for Chelsea, and the addition of the unorthodox twist of having to discern "orientation," as it were, had generally tossed the idea so far out of her comfort zone it may as well have landed on another continent.

She had a feeling, though, that Jocelyn was no stranger to such liaisons. Her coworker seemed to exhibit no inhibitions, nothing but grace and curiosity and openness, somehow maintaining what seemed an utmost sincerity in this world thought to be so full of falsity and manipulation. It was obvious Jocelyn loved the men to whom she catered professionally, but really, Chelsea reflected, Jocelyn seemed to love everybody.

"Mickey" was announced, and Chelsea descended the stairs from the dressing room to the stage. Like metal to a magnet, her eyes found Jocelyn instantly in the crowd. She was near the bar in the back, speaking with a well-dressed gentleman who stood up as Chelsea watched, stepping back to let Jocelyn lead him toward the VIP area.

Jocelyn turned her head toward the stage. Chelsea felt a jolt zip through her as her friend's eyes met hers, followed instantly by that brilliant snow-white smile Jocelyn never seemed to hold back. She winked and blew Chelsea a kiss just before she disappeared through the doorway of the VIP lounge.

Chelsea worked to catch her breath. She had wondered sometimes if her infatuation inadvertently helped her with business. Potential customers might appreciate the cause of the flush on her cheeks or the shimmer of moisture on her naked pussy as she twirled around the pole, never knowing they were the result of the stunning woman making the rounds in her trademark white seven-inch heels, the aura of perfection Chelsea saw in her emanating like a cloud of perfume.

As Chelsea dipped low now, focusing her gaze on the circle of customers surrounding the stage, she felt the blood rushing to her clit—but it wasn't because of the excitement of the spotlight, the men looking hungrily at her from the front row and back as far as the bar to the side of the stage. It was because of that kiss, the innocent gesture Jocelyn had undoubtedly offered with the same casualness she had her smile but that sent Chelsea's imagination into places wet with desire. Her mind whirled with images of Jocelyn's stunning dark hair thrown back as she thrust her bare breasts toward Chelsea's mouth, of Chelsea's fingers plunging deep into the hot recesses of her desire, her body—her soul.

A scattering of applause startled her from her reverie as her first song ended. Flushed and out of breath, she found herself in a position she didn't remember getting into, on her knees with her thighs splayed wide, her hands gripping her breasts. She could feel that her royal blue G-string was almost soaked through.

With a deep breath, she stood somewhat unsteadily and began her second song.

Alex pushed a drawer of the metal toolbox shut with a clang. "Want to grab dinner after we close?" he called to her across the service bay.

Chelsea finished replacing the distributor cap of the SUV whose hood she was under. "I have to work tonight," she grumbled. She must be one of the only people in the greater metropolitan area who disliked Fridays. Working both her jobs that day made it one she tended not to look forward to. "Which means in three hours I have to look like a model ready for a photo spread—as much as I can, anyway." Chelsea glowered at the SUV's engine, aware of the grease smeared on her sweat-covered neck and, as always when she was at the shop, caked under her nails and covering her hands.

"Well, right now you're a great big mess," Alex said cheerfully.

"Yeah, thanks," Chelsea muttered, emerging from under the hood and grabbing the rag from her back pocket. Knowing that Jocelyn wasn't working that night virtually eliminated all appeal of the prospect of going to work for another several hours after she got done at Carter's.

Alex had the rough, scruffy, dirty-blond look so many bad-boy fantasies seemed to be made of. Usually sporting a few days' beard, his hair sexily unkempt and just long enough to reach his eyes, the grease customarily smeared over his coveralls or the white T-shit he wore underneath completed the look. Chelsea had seen more than one woman linger a little longer than necessary as Alex went to work on her vehicle, running her eyes up and down his flawless physique and seeking, Chelsea suspected, another kind of service altogether.

"Where's Caroline tonight?" she asked, remembering Alex's invitation.

Alex turned away and walked back to the toolbox, stuffing his own rag in his pocket as he went. He didn't answer right away.

"She went to her parents' for the weekend."

Chelsea sent him a glance before picking up a wrench and returning to the SUV's engine. The volatile nature of Alex and Caroline's five-year relationship had culminated in what had seemed to be a constant on-again, off-again pattern for the last two. Chelsea surmised that they were probably in the midst of another one of their extended arguments.

"Well, I'm sorry I'm not available tonight," she said into the grime inches from her face. "I could do lunch tomorrow if you want."

"How's your mom doing?" Alex's voice came again.

Chelsea sighed. "Good question." The inquiry reminded her that she was probably overdue for a phone call to her mother, another thing she didn't look forward to. Tossing her wrench on the floor, she stood up and wiped her hands before lowering the hood of the SUV, watching as it fell closed with a thud.

Chelsea slept in the next day. She wasn't working at Carter's, and she didn't have to go to the Silver Dollar until evening. After making French toast for breakfast, she made her way back into the bedroom, flopped on the bed and stared at the phone.

Without thinking long enough to change her mind, she reached for it and punched in the number. As she listened to the ringing on the other end, her stomach suddenly swirled with sadness, and she found it hard to speak through the lump in her throat when her mother answered.

"Hi, Mom."

"Hello, Chelsea."

Chelsea repositioned herself on the bed, sitting up and bringing her legs toward her as she leaned back against the pillows.

"How are you feeling?" Chelsea's eyes dropped to the streaks of sunlight the open blinds stenciled across the floor as she listened to the dry response informing her that her mother felt tired and not much was different.

"But there's no reason to worry about me so much. I'll be fine."

Cheslea restrained a sigh. She was well aware that what that meant was that her mother felt neglected and was considering embarking on one of her famous guilt trips. Chelsea tried to recall the last conversation she'd had with her mother that didn't include one of these.

Her mother was still talking. "So anyway, it's just another test, and it probably won't tell him anything different than any of the other ones have."

"Yeah, but it's a good idea to listen to the doctor, Mom. I'm sure he knows what he's doing."

"Ha! Yeah, I'm sure he makes a lot of money knowing what he's doing, too. This test'll cost two hundred dollars. He must think the salary of a secretary is generous or something."

Chelsea closed her eyes briefly. "Mom, you know I'm helping you with your medical bills. Do what your doctor says."

There was a brief silence, and Chelsea narrowed her eyes as she sensed her mother's embarrassment. While she was usually pretty straightforward about accepting money—she thought it was an even trade after she'd worked so hard to raise Chelsea all by herself—sometimes it seemed to humble her.

"Mom?"

"Yes. Yes, I know that, Chelsea, and I appreciate it. This is all just such a nuisance. But I suppose I brought it on myself, running all those years trying to raise you without taking any time to take care of myself."

Chelsea looked at the ceiling. "I'll send you a check next weekend, Mom."

At the club that night, the conversation returned to her. Even at twenty-four, seven years after she had hightailed it out of her mother's house at age seventeen, Chelsea still sometimes felt like the little girl who could never seem to do what was needed to make her mother happy. Her mother had been one big mess of ignoring and smothering throughout her childhood, swinging back and forth between the two like a pendulum on a clock Chelsea never learned how to read. Early on Chelsea had stopped resenting the fact that she didn't have a father and focused on trying to elude her mother, who had managed to remind her constantly how hard it was to be a single parent, as if Chelsea had somehow asked to be born into the circumstance she was and held single-handed responsibility for the difficulty her mother perceived in her life.

The day Chelsea had found her mother in the kitchen to share the news that she'd gotten her first period, the response she'd received was, "I hope you don't think that means you're old enough to start having sex. Because if you ever get pregnant while you're living under my roof, you won't be living under it anymore." Her mother had emphasized the words with a sharp thrust of the knife into the block of cheddar she'd been slicing while Chelsea had stood stock-still, too stunned and mortified to say another word.

Chelsea wasn't prone to hilarity, but she chuckled dryly to herself now as she walked through the club, thinking about the clueless twelve-year-old girl she'd been and how ironic it was that she was a stripper now. It would be a few years after that discussion before she'd learn much about sex—before she started having it, but after she realized the interest she felt in girls as well as boys was not universal, to say the least, and began the process of grappling with that in the context of the small rural town where they lived. Had it not been for the blessedly open-minded mother of her best friend in high school, Chelsea had no idea how she would have traversed any of it. Especially since despite her mother's dire warnings—which would from then on become a theme filled with grave threats but no concrete infor-mation to speak of—the woman never gave her any informa-tion about birth control. It was thanks to Vanessa's mom that Chelsea had gotten on the pill before she needed to be and that she carried condoms in her purse to this day.

Not that she'd needed them much in recent years. Another irony. She was a stripper who hadn't had sex in six months.

A prospective customer caught her eye, and Chelsea shook her thoughts aside, giving him a smile as she started across the room and returned her attention to her work.

Chelsea did a double take as she noticed the lights on at the shop on her way home. She switched lanes and turned into the parking lot, spotting Alex's truck parked behind the building.

The door was locked, and Chelsea flipped through her keys and let herself in. She walked through the reception area back to the office.

"What are you doing here?" she asked Alex, who was sitting on the floor of the bay just beyond the office door, a beer in his hand.

He looked up. Chelsea couldn't tell if he was surprised to see her or not. He didn't answer, and Chelsea sat down on the concrete floor beside him.

Alex stared straight ahead. "Caroline came back tonight." He took a swig of his beer and paused for so long Chelsea was about to respond when he said, "She said it was just to get her stuff."

Chelsea lowered her head. She reached to rest her fingertips on the sleeve of Alex's T-shirt. "You two have worked things out before, Alex. She probably just wants some time to cool off."

"Nah...I think it's really done this time." Alex's voice held just enough restraint of the desolation Chelsea sensed at its base that suddenly, she knew he was right. The automatic words of encouragement she'd been about to offer died on her lips.

They sat silently for several moments. Chelsea looked at Alex as he took another swig. In profile, what looked like the sheen of tears covered his eyes as he lowered the bottle, and she reached and squeezed his shoulder, letting her hand rest there for several seconds.

After a while Alex hoisted his body up from the concrete. "Anyway, I should get home and start sorting things out." He wiped his hands on his jeans and looked down at her.

Chelsea didn't know if he meant literally as far as the items in his and Caroline's shared apartment or something less tangible. She stood as well, brushing off her skirt as she killed the garage lights and followed him into the office.

"Call me if you need anything," she said, as he picked up his keys.

Alex turned and kissed her. There was no question in it, no

introduction, no hesitance, yet no possessiveness, no demand, either. She wasn't even sure if he himself had anticipated it any more than she had. He kissed her with the same immediacy with which she returned it, neither of them, she suspected, really thinking about it at all—just doing something born of the moment neither of them had the energy to question or strong enough desire to resist.

Alex grabbed her, squeezing her body like a lifeline, turning and pulling her on top of him as he sat in the swivel chair, their kiss never breaking. The urgency Chelsea felt in Alex's actions wasn't about her, she knew, and there was an honesty in that, a vulnerability she found herself touched by. It was what he needed, and something about that pulled her in even as her body began to respond beyond anything her mind might have to say.

Her skirt came up, and Alex plunged his fingers into her. Chelsea's breath disappeared, abandon securing a sudden and unforeseen possession of her as Alex tore off her shirt and she held on to his in desperation, a wetness that surprised her spilling onto Alex's fingers as he touched her clit lightly with his thumb.

Maybe it was what they both needed.

She looked down and met his eyes, fierce in the darkness as he gripped her waist and pulled her tighter against him. Reaching between their bodies, she felt the hardness beneath his jeans and twisted away to pull open her purse on the desk. She snatched the long-neglected condom from its home in the front pocket, and Alex took it from her and ripped it open as she stood to give him room.

For a second, there was a pause. She stood above him, looking into his shining eyes in the muted darkness of the office. Alex breathed heavily, his gaze never leaving hers as they stared, suspended, in the eye of the hurricane for this instant unde-fined.

Then their lips were joined again, her body dropping onto his as Alex's fingers dug into her hips. She rode him frantically, his thumb back on her clit as her hands found their way to his hair and clutched desperate fistfuls as she started to come with a long, crescendoing moan she didn't recognize as coming from her. Alex gripped her harder, a strangled sound tearing from his throat, the pain it held pulling forth Chelsea's own as they hung on to each other through climax, the moment agony and ecstasy blended into one, surpassing all identity into pure being, reminding them only that they were alive—and that that was all they needed.

Neither of them moved as the descent began, heartbeats slowing and breath evening. Chelsea's eyes were closed against Alex's neck as she felt the reorientation to the mundane begin to infiltrate her consciousness. But as she stood, she felt the looseness of her body, a relaxation she couldn't remember last experiencing. Her breathing came literally easier as she exhaled the last of what had just been released and aligned involuntarily with a new groundedness her body seemed to own. She turned in the darkness to give Alex a hug and caught her breath when she felt, rather than saw, a similar alchemical energy in his eyes. What it meant for him she couldn't know, but she was aware beyond doubt that it could only be enriching.

Alex closed the door behind them as they stepped outside. The air felt lighter than she remembered.

GOA

Dena Hankins

Thomas and I waved to get Cybele's attention in the airport. When she grinned and headed toward us, I squeezed his hand in relief. We'd been worried about her state of mind. The full day of flying to get to Mumbai and then Goa beat the stuffing out of most people, and she'd been going through hard times. Cybele and Willa had split up after an eight-year marriage and the end had been excruciating for them both. Right after Cybele moved out, she had applied for a passport so she could get away from Baltimore. India was about far enough.

We exchanged long, tight hugs and gave each other smacking kisses on the lips.

Rather than stay in our tiny, one-room rental house, Cybele had insisted on having her own hotel room for the two weeks she'd be in Goa. We had arranged a good price at a place on the best beach. We reached the hotel quickly and took Cybele's luggage to her room. I produced her welcome present and handed it to her with a kiss on the cheek.

She took the rectangle of fabric between her hands and

looked up at me with a frown. "No, Molly. You shouldn't have. I know you're living close to the bone."

"Don't you worry about us, Cybele," said Thomas.

"We're good at budgeting, honey." I stroked her arm. "Open it."

"First we have to agree. I buy all meals and pay if we go out places."

Thomas dropped the drape over the open door leading outside to Colva Beach. Punjabi music beat softly from the bar out there. He came to Cybele and took her upper arms in his hands. Leaning down to meet her eyes, he spoke with quiet authority. "You can pay if you like when we go out, but you must accept our gifts with good grace."

Cybele nodded and pulled the tuck loose on the bundle. It unfolded in her hands, revealing two sarongs, one wrapped in the other. Cybele stroked the intricate wood-block dyes and the tension of maintaining a cheerful façade fell away. Her breathing roughened. She began to cry and Thomas gathered her up in his arms, tossing the fabric on the bed behind him.

I hugged her from behind. She held Thomas with one arm around his waist and reached to pull me closer with the other. "I'm so happy to be here," she said on a hiccup. "It's such a relief to be with people who love me."

Cybele turned in our embrace, pressing Thomas back against the wooden bedstead. She put both arms around me and leaned her forehead into my shoulder. Thomas wrapped his arms around us.

In Baltimore, we had gone out as a foursome. Cybele and Willa ate and drank with great appetites and we assumed they were also sensualists in other ways. When they split up, Cybele called me on Skype and poured her heart out. Willa didn't want sex. Cybele was faithful to her promise that she wouldn't sleep

with anyone else, but Willa couldn't believe her. When Cybele
told me that they hadn't made love in three years, I could hardly
believe it myself. It was Willa's suspicious, unreasonable jealousy that had ended their marriage as much as the discrepancy
in their sex drives.

Thomas and I talked about their breakup and how much we
each found Cybele sexy. We'd been poly for ten years and were
accustomed to honesty about our attractions to other people. It
had been a while since I'd been with another woman, though,
and I was turned on by Cybele's soft, round body against mine.
Standing in the hotel room with jasmine scenting the air, holding
Cybele close, I met Thomas's eyes and knew that he was experiencing the same sexual response I was.

I raised an eyebrow at Thomas and sighed. This was the
emotional turmoil we had expected, and I wouldn't take advantage of her volatile state. Thomas wasn't even sure she would be
interested in him. She'd been nineteen when she'd last slept with
a man. She and Thomas were the same age, forty-two, so that
was a long time dedicated only to women.

While Thomas and I held our silent conversation, Cybele
stirred. Her breasts rubbed against mine and my expression
turned wry. Thomas smiled at me and raised one hand to stroke
my hair. Then Cybele did the unexpected.

She kissed my collarbone. She nipped at the thin skin there
and ran her tongue along the hollow. My eyes widened. Cybele
raised her head and I looked down. Before I could say a word,
she kissed me.

This kiss was a soft-lipped, soft-tongued excursion into my
mouth, and I hummed with surprised pleasure. Plunged deep
into heat and wet, we stroked our tongues together, nibbled and
sucked on each other's lips. My hands went to her shoulders and
grasped hard.

Then I realized that Cybele was twisting her hips back and forth, slowly and sinuously. But it wasn't for my benefit. She rubbed her ass against Thomas's cock, and his arms turned to iron around her.

I broke the kiss with a gasp. Panting, I pulled away. Cybele allowed me to slide from her arms. Though I gained a foot of distance, I was riveted by the sight before me.

Cybele raised an arm and hooked it behind Thomas's neck. She leaned back against his chest and kept rotating her hips against his cock. Her other arm reached for his hip, and his breathing became labored. His hands were fisted in her shirt at her sides as though he was fighting the urge to grab her tightly.

I stood, mouth open and dazed by hunger, one hand on my chest and the other on my belly. I was flooded with heat and my pussy was drenched. Thomas knew, of course. Cybele could tell as well, though, for she smiled with delight and I saw, for the first time since she'd arrived, the old life and gleam in her eyes.

"What do you want, Cybele?" I had to ask.

"I want to fuck you." Her words made me shiver. "I want you to fuck me. I want to fuck your husband. I want to feel his cock in me and eat your pussy. I want to be in this room with you both, naked and doing whatever feels good. I've been fantasizing about this since I bought my tickets."

With those words, Thomas and I looked at each other. My skin was tight over my cheekbones and my smile felt predatory, a wolfish baring of teeth in anticipation of satisfying my appetites. Cybele leaned back against Thomas's chest again and he wrapped himself around her. He took a great big bite of her shoulder, gnawing on her muscles where they climbed her neck. His hands went to her breasts and massaged them.

I stepped closer and raised her chin. Her head fell to the side so Thomas could keep devouring her neck but her eyes rose to meet mine. "You are so damn sexy. Your lips and your tits. I've stared at your waist and your hips every time you've walked in front of me for years now. I want to touch you everywhere."

Cybele's breasts were heaving with her rapid breaths and her eyes were half-covered by heavy lids. I began unbuttoning her shirt from the top, revealing the cleavage I had seen so many times. When I had revealed them down to the rosette between her bra cups, I couldn't resist. I buried my face in her breasts, holding them tight from the sides and nuzzling, nipping, licking their curves. Pulling away, I made quick work of the rest of the buttons and her shirt fell away from her breasts.

I was usually patient, with the sensualist's desire to stretch out every moment. In this moment, though, I wanted in. I fell to my knees. I wanted to feel and taste Cybele's pussy so badly that I grabbed the hem of her skirt and gathered the fabric up, tucking it into the waistband. Looking upward, I saw her head tilted back, her shirt agape, her bra straining to hold her burgeoning breasts. I stripped her panties off without ceremony and buried my face in her pussy.

She was so wet! I had never felt so much pussy juice, dripping from her furred lips down the insides of her thighs. I slid right into her, my nose and chin and tongue suddenly surrounded by slippery, satiny tissues, puffy and open. I pulled her ornate inner lips into my mouth, sucking, trying to engulf her entire pussy in my mouth. My nose bumped against her clit and I found the entrance to her cunt with one thumb. The combination of sensations made her knees collapse and she would have fallen had Thomas not held her up.

Thomas spread his legs and whispered in her ear. "Raise your leg." When she complied, he hooked an arm under her thigh and said, "Now the other one." Legs braced wide, with much of his weight on the bedstead, Thomas held Cybele's legs high and open. I could see his cock straining at his fly, right under her spread asscheeks. I stroked my fingernails down the backs of her thighs and she shuddered and moaned.

I dove back in, thrusting a thumb into her pussy. I licked and sucked her clit, standing proud from under its hood. Cybele jerked in Thomas's arms and cried out. Her hands went to her own breasts, grabbing the lace-covered flesh. Thomas groaned at the sight and said, "That's right, Cybele. Touch them."

My face was deep in crinkly hair and dripping pussy juice. I couldn't believe how much lubrication Cybele was making. She smelled and felt so fucking sexy that I wanted to bottle her essence and keep it around for after she was gone.

I focused down to the exposed head of her clit, sucking hard and flicking my tongue up and down over it. She flinched and I switched to a softer swirl, which she met with a rotation of her hips. I could see her abdominal muscles working under the soft layer of her belly fat and Thomas's arms clenching to keep her from bouncing right out of them. The walls of her pussy pulsed around my thrusting thumb.

Then she screamed. A long, loud ululation filled the hotel room as I stayed with her jerking, jumping pussy. I drank her juices and felt them pour down my chin onto my cotton top. Cybele's face and chest turned red and her clit tried to hide. I was determined to wring every bit I could from her and I nuzzled her clit hood until she sagged weakly in Thomas's arms.

I pulled my hand from her pussy and knelt back on my heels, a satisfied grin on my face. Thomas shifted around the corner of the bedstead and sat with Cybele in his lap, legs draped over his. I stood up and got a condom, then walked between their legs. "Lie back," I told him softly.

When he did, I undid his jeans and tugged them down with his underwear. He bounced slightly to help, and Cybele moaned in protest at the motion. Thomas's cock was hard and silky, with veins pulsing just under the skin. I licked the wedge-shaped tip. All I could smell was pussy, but Thomas's taste came through a bit, satisfying me for the moment.

I unrolled the condom over his cock and guided it to the entrance of Cybele's pussy. It was so tight on my relatively small thumb that I worried about her ability to accommodate his thickness. She and I had gone sex toy shopping together, and she'd confided that she missed penetration. Though I wondered why she didn't get something to use by herself, it had remained another mysterious aspect of her sexual deal with Willa.

When the tip of his cock touched her pussy, he jerked and so did she. Cybele murmured and I leaned over her to hear.

"Yes," she mumbled. "Yes. Please."

Her swollen pussy pulled in with a clench of her muscles and opened up a tiny bit when she relaxed. I guided Thomas's cock back to her entrance and she sighed when it slipped a little way inside. Even the unlubed condom was drenched in seconds and I watched, fascinated, as Thomas made minuscule motions with his hips, pushing his cock into her less than an inch and then pulling out to barely touch her again.

Cybele's legs were still spread and held by Thomas's hands. I stroked Cybele's bare belly. Her diaphragm expanded under my hand as she fought for breath. Thomas was barely an inch inside. I stroked his iron-hard thighs and he shook hard, moving his cock in her and making them both groan. She was so small.

Without touching Thomas, who was overstimulated as it was, I placed my fingertips over Cybele's clit. She moaned and pressed down on his cock at my touch, so I made a slow circle. I rose to my knees beside them and kept one hand in her bush while I brought my mouth to her tits. Cybele moaned low, an alto reaching the bottom of her range, and I knew we were on the right track.

Thomas's cock stretched Cybele wide open. Her clit stood out, stark and stiff, and I cupped it with my fingers, keeping my caresses light and slow.

Thomas sank into her with unutterable slowness to almost half of his length. Cybele whimpered at being stretched so tight. She put her hands behind her, on either side of his chest, and pushed herself up a bit. I didn't take my hand from her clit. This new angle slipped him inside another inch and she cried out. "Oh, my god. I don't know if I can take it." She looked at me wildly and I smiled.

"You don't have to do anything, baby. Just relax and enjoy." I smoothed her hair.

Cybele's eyes dilated and she brought her head toward me for a kiss. We meshed our mouths tightly. I slipped her shirt from her shoulders and she lifted her arm to let it slide off. Again she slipped farther onto Thomas and cried out. This time Thomas flinched hard. He grated, "God, Cybele. You're so tight it hurts. I can't move at all without you clenching even tighter."

"I'm sorry." Cybele was nearly sobbing.

"Please, don't apologize." His voice had a dark humor to it. "We'll make it work or we'll switch to something else."

I unhooked her bra. When Cybele sat up to bring her arms forward, she panted and flexed her belly. I pulled her bra off quickly and she fell back against his chest.

When Thomas groaned, I took a quick look. Cybele had pulled nearly off his cock again and she started circling her hips. I grinned and encouraged her. "You want it back now, don't you? You're hungry for that cock, after all. You had half of it and now a little bit won't do it. Come on, Cybele. Take it and use it." While I growled the words in her ear, I also put my hand back on her clit and cupped one of her breasts, rubbing the hard nipple with my thumb.

Cybele bucked and Thomas's cock slipped out. I pushed it against her clit and she sobbed. "Put it back in me. I want it in me. You're right. Molly, I need it."

I pushed down and slipped it back into her softened flesh. Now somewhat accustomed to his thickness, Cybele took an inch right away. She levered herself back up onto her hands and angled for more. Thomas grabbed her hips and she sat up all the way. With closed eyes and a rapturous face, Cybele slid back and forth on it, taking a little more each time. She opened her eyes and looked at me pleadingly. "Help me. Please, Molly."

I got down on my knees again, between Thomas's thighs. Cybele braced her hands behind her on Thomas's chest and tried to press down on him harder. "Please, Molly, can you lick me?" I laid my tongue on her clit.

Cybele lifted her hips, pressing her clit into my tongue, and lowered them to impale herself farther on Thomas. As she set up a rhythm, fucking my face, fucking his cock, Thomas grunted at each downswing. She softened more and he was all the way in, his balls pressed under my chin. Cybele froze.

"What do you want?" he growled.

"Fuck me," she demanded.

Thomas pulled his hips down and then slid back up. Flexing his hips and ass, Thomas fucked Cybele slowly while I kept a finger on her clit. I watched the slide of his cock and Cybele's pussy reddened more and more. She started moving with him and I sat on the bed beside her. I took her nipple in my mouth and sucked while setting up a rhythm with my fingers that matched the motion of their hips. Cybele cried out again and again, as though there was too much sensation, but she didn't back away from it. She fucked herself down on Thomas's cock until she came, pulling herself almost off him, gushing. She drenched Thomas and quivered while she slowly, slowly slipped back down on him.

Thomas jerked. "Oh, please, don't squeeze me like that. I don't want to come yet."

Cybele slid off him and to the side, shoving her skirt down and off. I leaned over Thomas and checked in with him. He gave me a grimace and then a smile. I kissed him and his cock jumped, making Cybele laugh.

I kissed Thomas again, in the way we loved. Lots of lip, a little tongue, a little tooth. He put one hand on my breast and the other on Cybele's thigh. I put my hand on his chest and realized he was still wearing his light cotton shirt.

I pulled away, laughing. Sure enough, he also had his pants around his ankles. "Let's get you out of those clothes," I said.

"Tit for tat," he replied.

"Sure." I helped him pull his shirt off and kissed the point of his shoulder, lightly scratching his back.

"Mmm-hmm," he hummed, shaking his pants from his feet.

Cybele looked sleepy, lying on her side with her head propped in her hand.

"You sure you don't want to take a nap?" I asked. "We could take this home for now."

"No way," she replied. "I don't want to miss a minute."

I grinned at her and planted my feet wide. Playing stripper, I swayed my hips and cupped my breasts, bending closer to her. She grinned at my antics and I turned in a circle.

Cybele and I had very similar bodies—large breasts, full hips, narrow waists, though not at all skinny. Her skin was finer than mine. My muscles were stronger. I danced to the hint of bhangra music that wafted through the open door to the beach. Sexy, sexy music. I pulled my top off and slipped out of my shorts, dancing for a moment in my bra and panties. I drew out the revelation of my breasts, turning around at the last second to hide them a moment longer. Tucking my thumbs in the waist of my panties, I lowered them slowly over my round asscheeks and bent in half, knees straight, to drop them to my feet.

As they hit the floor, a narrow face pressed into my pussy from the back. I spread my legs and touched my fingers to the floor in front of me for balance. Cybele squeezed my buttcheeks and nibbled at the tops of my thighs. She pulled away and said, "Lie down on the bed, face up."

I joined Thomas on the bed. Cybele followed me down, attacking my pussy like I was going to push her away. Tenderness welled in me at the thought of Willa turning her down year after year.

Cybele brought her teeth into the action and the sharp little bites freaked me out. I wasn't sure I could take them and I looked at Thomas with wide eyes. He understood and moved behind Cybele, raising her hips and sliding his cock into her tight pussy. His face was stiff with concentration, his eyes closed and his hands on her hips. Cybele moaned against my clit. The overwhelming sensation of being fucked from behind distracted her and she rubbed her face in my pussy without plan or technique. As a slow, easy rhythm got established between them, Cybele took to licking me again, giving me the stimulation that I wanted. She used her lips and tongue and, yes, her teeth, but now she monitored my responses and drove me quickly up to the peak of orgasm.

I shivered, clutching her head to me, and chanted, "Yes, yes, yes." Her tongue surged against my clit with the thrusting of Thomas's cock and she made little circles. The combination drove me over the edge and waves broke through my body.

Thomas picked up the power of his thrusts and fucked Cybele

into me. She slid up my body, straddling my hips. Thomas followed and Cybele kissed me hard, tasting of my pussy. She grabbed my tits and squeezed them, moaning into my mouth as Thomas angled down and pushed at her G-spot. I reached a hand between our hips and found her clit with my middle finger. Cybele squeezed my tits harder in each hand and kissed me fiercely. She flexed into Thomas's thrusts and I rubbed her clit until she froze and came.

Thomas kept thrusting and she sobbed again and again. She moved higher and higher on my body from the force of Thomas's pounding. Her breasts came within reach and I sucked in one of her nipples. She was still coming, or perhaps coming again; my fingertips felt her pussy flex around Thomas. I caught his balls in my palm, holding them against his body and squeezing them to the rhythm of his thrusts.

Thomas shouted and groaned, jerking into Cybele's body again and again. She quivered over me, her nipple in my mouth and her pussy dripping over my belly. Thomas's legs shook from the strain of the angle he was holding. Finally, he pulled out and collapsed beside us, pulling off the full condom.

We all gasped for air, sweaty and stunned. Cybele had the first word. "Wow."

Thomas nodded and I tried to laugh, but I was too weak to move even that much under Cybele. She slid down me, spreading her juices over my belly and making me clench again. Moving between Thomas and me, Cybele slipped into Thomas's embrace and put one hand on my wet hip.

When I could speak, I asked with my eyes closed, "How are you doing, Cybele? Do you need a nap or some food?"

"I slept on the plane," she replied, her voice muffled by Thomas's chest. "And if I get hungry, I'll order room service." She sighed.

"Sounds good to me," said Thomas.

I looked over at him and reached out. Our hands met and I mouthed, "I love you."

He did the same and then stretched, long and hard, like a cat. Cybele was dislodged in the process and she spoke with surprise. "Wow, I didn't know you could do that."

I looked at her and then down. Thomas was hard again. I laughed and kissed her back. "There are a lot of things you don't know about us."

Cybele turned over to look at me. "I can't wait to learn."

THE ROBBER GIRL

Lori Selke

The robber girl owns thirteen knives. Twelve, actually, for one is a straight razor. They all have names. "This one's Judith," she says, pulling the blade along the sharpening stone. "This one's Salome. Jezebel, Delilah, Shemamah the Desolate, Mara the Bitter," she recites, running her fingers along the edge of each blade. "They are my daughters; they are my coven."

"You can trust steel," she tells Gerda. "With steel, you know where you stand. It's glass that's treacherous, like water; it looks placid, but it bites. Steel is hot, glass is ice. But you already know all about that, don't you?"

"I could pierce your heart with steel the way she pierced Kay's heart with glass," she whispers to Gerda one night in bed. "I could turn you hard and hot, the way she turned him hard and cold. I could make you forget him. I could turn your heart."

"Yes, you could," Gerda replies, her breath coming in gasps. "Oh, oh, yes, you could."

"I can feel the furnace inside you," the robber girl whispers. "I know how to stoke it."

"Yes," Gerda says, and kisses her lover hard. Their conversation stops for the night.

By day, the robber girl teaches Gerda how to ride a horse, how to pick a lock, how to keep a band of unruly men in line. She is the Robber Queen.

"They think you're pretty," the robber girl says. "That's because you are."

Gerda blushes.

"Your pretty face can be a liability, or it can be a tool," the robber girl says. "I myself am plain. I have learned to use other tools." Her hand strays to Gerda's waist. "Let the men admire you. Let them do you little favors. Do them favors in return. They will be loyal as dogs. But don't give them everything," she adds. "Leave them wanting more."

She leans in to whisper in Gerda's ear. "Right now, what they want is you. But I won't let them have what they want. You are my prize." Her hand pinches Gerda's butt. Gerda jumps. "But I will let them look. They will drink in your face like a draft from a well. They will know that you please me, and that will please them, too."

"Do you ever let them touch you?" Gerda asks, ducking her head into the robber girl's pungent armpit after she speaks.

"Sometimes," the robber girls admits. She looks down at her blushing lover. "Did you ever let Kay?"

"Sometimes," Gerda admits.

"He wasn't really my brother."

The robber girl nods. Her mouth is full; she and Gerda are sharing a dinner bought with stolen coin.

"People thought we were brother and sister because we looked so much alike. It was probably our hair," Gerda said, fingering her smooth blonde braid. "And our eyes." Her eyes are a guileless blue. "But we weren't related."

"He was your lover," the robber girl states.

"My first," Gerda says.

The robber girl nods and fills her mouth with roast chicken. Gravy spots her chin, her shirt.

"You're my second," Gerda says.

The robber girl grins. Gerda wipes the gravy from her chin with a kiss.

Gerda remembers the morning the robber girl found her.

She was wearing leather. Black leather, the crevices caked with dust from the road. Leather pants. Leather vest that left her arms bare. Her skin was dark, a deep brown; not the brown of a crust of fresh-baked bread, but the bronze of temple idols. Her hair was black, and long; it hung free past her shoulders, tangled by the wind. Her eyes, too, were black.

Her smell was strong; it mingled with the scent of the horse she rode. It was a smell both pungent and clean.

"I could have killed you, when we first found you," the robber girl says. "But you were too pretty. I could have let my men have their way with you, but I stopped them. We thought you were a princess. You were wearing a princess's clothes."

"They were a gift," Gerda says.

"From your lover?" the robber girl sneers.

Gerda laughs. "No. You know you are my first."

"Your first woman," the robber girl corrects.

"Yes," Gerda says soberly.

* * *

The robber girl's hands are on Gerda's breasts, her thighs, the cleft between her legs. They are restless, roaming. Like the robber girl, they cannot settle down.

"I cannot erase his traces from your body," the robber girl says.

"He took my virginity," Gerda confirms.

"I cannot erase his impression upon your heart."

"He broke it."

"I can never be first. I can never restore you." The robber girl rolls on her side, away from Gerda.

Gerda reaches out to touch her shoulder, then her buttock. "Do you love only broken things?" she says.

The robber girl turns and grins over her shoulder, then grabs Gerda by the shoulders and kisses her until her lips bruise. "Yes," she replies. "I like broken things best of all. I have strong hands; they take to mending well."

"You cannot mend the break," Gerda replies, "but you can stitch the seam."

"I like girls with scars," the robber girl says, and bites Gerda's nipple. Gerda laughs and falls into her arms.

"If I find him, I will kill him," the robber girl says. "I will kill him for hurting you."

In bed one night, she puts a knife against Gerda's throat. "This is Salome," she says. "Small but sharp. Say her name."

"Salome."

"Kiss her."

Gerda kisses the tip of the blade.

The robber girl draws the tip down Gerda's body, through the notch in her throat, along the breastbone. She stops at her heart. "Salome likes to slip between the ribs of her victims," the robber girl says. She pushes against Gerda's flesh until Gerda goes rigid. Then the robber girl pulls the knife down her abdomen, past her navel. Then she sheathes the blade.

She draws her razor. "My head was shaved once," she says, holding the edge near Gerda's ear. "As a punishment. They sought to make me ugly and ashamed. Ashamed of my wantonness, my free ways." The robber girl grins and bites Gerda's earlobe. Gerda squeaks. "But do you know what? I liked it. Would you like it? All your pretty golden locks, shorn away? No more tangles in the morning. No more dubious looks from men." She wraps her hand in Gerda's hair and tugs. "No more convenient handhold. You could learn to be like me. I would teach you the names of my blades and the ways of my art. My art with men, and with women. The art of commanding a band of brigands. The art of robbing. The arts of love."

"If you did that," Gerda whispers, "I would no longer be your lover, but your daughter."

"Yes," the robber girl replies. "You would be sharp, like my blades."

"You like me soft," Gerda says. "You like me vulnerable."

"Yes," the robber girl says, and bites Gerda's neck. Gerda gasps and struggles to continue.

"I want to be your lover," she says. "Not your protégé."

"You will leave me," the robber girl says, and pushes Gerda's face into the blankets. She kicks Gerda's knees apart and works her hand inside. Her touch is rough.

Gerda persists. "Daughters leave, too," she says. "Oh."

"I could make you a toy," the robber girl whispers fiercely in her ear, her hand working all of Gerda's tender parts. Gerda's moisture floods out of her and pools in the robber girl's palm. "A plaything. A possession. I could put a collar and a leash upon you, hitch you to my wagon like a pet. Use your tongue

to please me, your dumb unspeaking tongue." The robber girl
rocks her hips above Gerda's buttocks. "Then you would never
leave me."

"But you would tire of me," Gerda says. Tears squeeze from
the corners of her eyes. Her thighs clench around the robber
girl's wrist.

The robber girl's wrist twists, finds the spot that makes
Gerda cry in earnest now, in joy and in pain. Gerda howls her
tormented pleasure into the dense night.

"You're right," the robber girl says as Gerda screams. "I
would tire of a toy. I would break it. But I would never break
you."

Later, after they have put the lamp out, the robber girl whispers into Gerda's ear. "You will leave me anyway, daughter or
no. You will leave to find Kay."

Gerda says nothing. Her breathing is even and deep.

"I will give you a knife, to cut out his heart."

"To cut out the cold splinter, you mean," Gerda says. She
rolls over and strokes her lover's cheek.

"As you choose," the robber girl says, and grasps her wrist.
She kisses it tenderly, and lies back down again.

The night before they visit a metalsmith in town, the robber girl
performs the ritual again. "This is Judith," she says, holding the
blade to Gerda's lips. "Kiss it." Gerda obeys. "The real Judith
cut off the head of a king," the robber girls says, her hand on
Gerda's neck, pinning her to the sleeping pallet spread over the
hard ground.

Gerda opens her mouth; the robber girl slips the blade inside.
"Suck it," she says. Gerda obeys. The robber girl grinds her hips
against Gerda's thigh; her mouth tears at Gerda's nipples, which
are exposed to the cold air. Her mouth ravages Gerda's throat.

Still Gerda sucks, eyes closed, her body held perfectly rigid and still. Finally, the robber girl withdraws the blade. Carefully, deliberately, she nicks Gerda's lower lip. Gerda flinches at the touch. The robber girl licks the blood away and smiles. She pricks herself, just above the notch of her collarbone, and presses Gerda's head against it so that Gerda may taste the salty flow as well. As Gerda licks and suckles like a puppy, the robber girl rummages between Gerda's thighs until she finds her wetness. Her touch is not gentle, but it causes Gerda to moan. "I would like to sheathe my blade in you," the robber girl whispers as she chews on Gerda's ear. "In your lovely wet hole, I would like to bury myself. Your slick scabbard. Would you take it for me? Would you sheathe my sharpness?"

"Yes," Gerda says with a gasp. The robber girl buries her hand in Gerda's moist space.

"If you are wet enough, soft enough, I cannot harm you," the robber girl breathes. "If you yield, I cannot conquer. You will melt away at my touch, I will leave you unscathed."

"No," Gerda says.

"You want me to scar you, to mar your pretty, soft flesh."

"Yes," Gerda says.

The robber girl points Judith at the spot below Gerda's navel, just above her mons. She pushes and pushes until the blood wells up around the tip of the blade.

"A sharp blade leaves a cut that heals," the robber girl says. "Only a dull blade marks." She removes the knife, smears the blood on her palm and gives it to Gerda to lick clean. "I cannot mark you. I will pass through your life like a clean cut. It will sting; it will heal."

Gerda answers her by nuzzling the robber girl's breast, by allowing the girl to pull her hair, pinch her flesh, be as rough and as ruthless as she wishes with Gerda's body. She is left with bite marks, with scratches and bruises, with soreness and wetness. They are both left fulfilled.

In the morning, the robber girl buys a knife for Gerda. It is a plain knife with a bone handle. The robber girl teaches her how to sharpen and care for it. Then she teaches Gerda how to fight with it. How to make a bold challenge, and how to deftly slip it between someone's ribs. She spars with Gerda.

"Name the knife," the robber girl commands one day. "All knives have names."

"How do you know a knife's name?" Gerda says.

"Ask it."

Gerda thinks, the blade is a tongue, it will speak to me. But her knife is silent, though she asks every night.

She takes to whispering names to her knife in the darkness. "Athaliah, Zillah, Rahab, Tamar." The knife is still and cold in her hand.

When, one day, Gerda parries her strike and flips the knife out of the robber girl's hands, she laughs, grabs Gerda's wrist and kisses it.

"You have bested me today," the robber girl says. "Now you must be on your way. Go. Find your lover, Kay. Cut out his heart. Slit his queen's snowy throat. When you return to me, I will lick his blood from your hands. I will lick you clean."

Gerda sheathes her knife in her boot. "You will find another broken thing to nurse to health, to mend," says Gerda sadly.

"No," says the robber girl. "I will wait for you to return. Not as my daughter, not as my toy, but as my equal. My fierce, wild lover. My vengeance-seeker. My murderess." She spoke the words as endearments. "I look forward to fearing your hands," she said. "As men fear mine."

"I don't fear your hands," says Gerda.

"And that is why you must go."

So she set Gerda on the road, with a fierce kiss and a gift of gold, and a promise elicited to return. And it wasn't until Gerda was well away from the camp that she realized she had never even learned the robber girl's name.

THE ADULTERERS

Penelope Friday

You open the door to Markus's office, knowing he is still there, knowing he will be sitting in the solid chair behind his desk.

"Still here?" he asks.

You smile at him suggestively. "Yes." You say nothing more. Although you are fairly confident about what will happen next, you are going to leave it to him. No need to make a fool of yourself unnecessarily.

"Can I help you with anything?" he asks.

"I rather thought it might be the other way around," you say coyly.

"What?"

"You know what."

He is unable to keep from smirking, and you know you were right. He wants you. He wants you, and he has always intended to have you. You have just made it easy for him.

"I didn't know you felt that way."

"Didn't you?" you ask.

You slide farther into the room, walking around the desk so that you are standing just by him. The air-conditioning has made your nipples stand out; the thin blouse you are wearing does nothing to conceal this. Why should it, when it was chosen precisely for this purpose?

"Gennie…"

"Shh." You press a finger to his lips then trail it down his body as you kneel before him. "Tell me you don't want this," you say.

He is silent, and you smile, all feminine confidence. You rest a hand on his thigh and look up at him from your new position. He looks a little guilty, a touch ashamed…and so he should. He has a wife waiting for him at home, someone who loves him, someone he professes to love. But he's here with you, like this. You lean forward, and his lips are slightly apart, his eyes glazed, as he shuffles forward on his seat, allowing you to take the zip of his jeans between your teeth and pull it down. His underwear is concealing his flesh—more or less—but it does nothing to hide the bulge, the erect cock waiting to be unleashed. You give him one last chance to say no, to pull away. He doesn't take it.

Your fingers are gentle as you rearrange his pants to let his cock spring free. It is thicker than you'd imagined when you'd considered seducing him, a dark red, altogether more real than any imaginings. When you lick it tentatively, he groans and shifts in his chair. The noise is guttural, animalistic, as if you've stripped him down just to this, so that he is all body and no mind, no higher intelligence, no emotion even.

"Shall I stop?" you whisper.

For an answer, he curls his fingers into your hair, thrusting your face toward his groin. Apparently not. You place kisses down his length, teasing him. You know he wants you to take him in, take that fat cock between your lips and swallow it whole. He must wait for that: this is your show, and you will do it your way. You run your tongue around his balls, taking pleasure in the difference in texture between the wrinkled sac and his full, hard cock. You kiss your way back up to the tip and then—oh, very well. He has borne with your teasing, and he shall have his reward. You open your mouth and guide him inside; he hisses on an indrawn breath as you do so.

So warm. So hot in your mouth, as if he has heated his cock especially for your pleasure. For a second you close your eyes; sometimes it feels as if you can experience more deeply without the distraction of sight. But you want to remember what he looks like—you want to remember every single thing about what you're doing, so that later...

Later can wait.

For now, you are going to concentrate all your attention on Markus, and it doesn't sound like he's going to object to that. You swirl your tongue around his erection, as if licking an ice-cream cone. Then you suck him in deeper, deeper—as far as you can. He fills you totally, and you find yourself salivating, just as if he really is some much-desired food. Your hand is on his thigh, and you can feel as he tenses his muscles, trying not to thrust in and out of you. You have to admire his self-restraint. He begins to speak, possibly to distract himself from the urgency of his need.

"I thought"—his voice is unsteady—"you did girls."

You slowly suck yourself free of his cock, replacing mouth with hand on his saliva-slicked erection. Part of the reason, you've always suspected, that he's been so desperate to fuck you is because he can't stand the idea that you'd prefer a woman to him.

"Who says I don't?" you murmur.

"But I'm..."

"Are you complaining?" You up the pace with your hand on his cock.

"No."

He says no more, his breathing getting faster with your increased hand speed. He smells of sweat and precome; looking up, you can see a bead of perspiration sliding down the side of his face. Sex makes men strangely vulnerable; you've never seen Markus look so exposed, in more than the obvious sense. You move your mouth down again, suckling on the end of his cock while your hand continues to rub up and down. There is a sudden hitch in his breathing, and then his prick twitches in your grip, spurting so much semen into your mouth that although you swallow, some dribbles down your chin. When he returns to normal, he has the grace to look a little embarrassed, perhaps a bit ashamed.

"Gennie, I..."

"You don't need to say anything." You wipe your chin, get to your feet again. "No need."

There is a half smile on his face as you say this, as if he only spoke to get this reaction from you.

"See you around, Markus," you say huskily, and are gone before he can speak another word.

As you walk to your car, you press a number into your mobile phone, holding it up to your ear.

Within seconds, the call has been answered. With one word: "Well?"

Kiera has been your best friend since childhood. If Markus had spent more time at home with his wife, less time at the office, he might have known that.

"Yes."

"He took the bait?"

"Yes," you say again.

Kiera sighs. Somewhere inside her, you suspect, she still loves him. But she needed to know. Needed to be *sure*. And you were the only person she could ask. It feels like a betrayal, just a little, even though it was her request.

"I'm sorry," you say.

And Kiera is herself again, strong and confident. "I'm not," she says firmly.

You can imagine the proud little lift of her head as she says the words, the same one she wore when she'd marched into a new school as a teenager, looking around and challenging people to like her or not as they wished. You had liked her—loved her— on sight. You still do.

"Kiera…"

She interrupts you, unexpectedly. "Gennie…I've always been too scared before. Markus seemed the safer option—a man, security. You've been the brave one, willing to say it aloud."

"Say what?" you ask, wondering whether she can possibly mean what it sounds like, trying not to give in to that treacherous emotion, hope.

"Queer." You can hear her hesitation over the phone line. "I always have been, you know."

You didn't know. You never knew—*never*—that she felt this way. You've known her for more than a decade, and you never realized.

"If you can say it, I can," she says, uncertainly. Then, "If Markus can have sex with someone else, I can, too." Then, most uncertainly of all, "You once said…"

"Yes," you say, quickly. You'd once told her you loved her; she had seemed frozen to the spot, you thought, appalled. It seems her emotion had been something very different. In another woman you might think this was her attempt at revenge on Markus, but Kiera is not like that. Has never been like that.

"Come round, Gennie?" she asks.

"Yes," you say again.

Ten minutes later, you are in her arms. Coming to her straight from her husband seems surreal; coming home to Kiera, however, seems almost frighteningly right. Amazingly, she feels the same.

"Why did I ever hesitate?" she asks, kissing your cheek, kissing your lips, kissing your neck.

"I don't know," you murmur, running your hands over her shoulders, down her back, cupping her beautiful ass.

She giggles. "Me neither. Gennie, come to bed."

A request you would never refuse. You don't let go of each other as you mount the stairs, Kiera in front holding your hand, turning to kiss you every few steps. Every time she turns, you undo another button on her blouse, until her silky bra is the only barrier between you and her small, high breasts. As you reach the bedroom, you slide a hand round to unclip the bra, and Kiera shrugs her blouse and bra off together. She is beautiful. Your touch is gentle as you reach out to stroke the curves of her breast, to rub the pad of your thumb across her nipple. She makes a small humming noise of pleasure, her head falling forward onto your shoulder.

"Good?" you ask.

"Good." She slides her hands inside the waistband of your trousers, pinching your ass. "Very good."

You both fall onto the bed, a tangle of bodies. Kiera pushes your trousers down and off and reaches a hand between your legs. You are already wet for her. You think of Markus, who just took and made no effort to reciprocate. Kiera deserves better than him. Her fingers rub tentatively against your clit, her eyes searching your face. You are her first, you realize—the first woman she has ever taken to bed. Yet for a novice she is amazingly good; you find yourself squirming a little under her touch, and you lean in for another kiss.

"I love you," you whisper. "I love you."

"I know." She kisses you back with increasing passion. "Me, too."

You wriggle down her body to suck on her nipples, first one and then the other. Kiera flops back on the bed, her hair spreading across the white linen pillowcase and forming a halo around her head. You unzip her skirt and slip a couple of fingers inside her panties—inside *her*.

"Oh," she says, then "*Oh*," again as you crook your fingers, playing in the warm softness of her pussy. You slip your whole hand inside her knickers, pressing the palm against her clit as you continue to move your fingers. She gives a happy sigh, but after a little she places her hand on top of yours. "Wait."

"What is it?"

Her eyes have a brightness you've not seen there before. "I want to touch you, too," she says huskily.

"Darling."

"I want to touch you everywhere."

Her hands run all over your body; she pulls you on top of her so that you are rubbing up against her. You've never imagined anything as magical as this. And when you look at Kiera's face, you can't do anything but believe that she is happy, that she really does want this—wants you. She kisses you, and she is laughing and crying, and you realize you are crying, too. Then you begin to move your fingers inside her again, and she has her hands on your breasts and she is coming, falling over that cliff of orgasm in joyous abandon.

You both look up, and see Markus standing in the doorway. He doesn't look happy. You look back at Kiera. She does—and as far as you're concerned, that's always been all that matters.

SUNSET

Logan Belle

After dinner they walked across the street to the pool at the Standard Hotel. This, after yet another argument. The argument was stupid—some of theirs were, remarkably so. And yet the latest argument started her thinking that maybe the relationship had run its course.

It wasn't quite dark yet, but the pool was quiet. Meg felt overdressed in her button-down shirt and pleated skirt. She knew that no matter how often she visited L.A., she would never convert to the dress code: the T-shirts cut strategically to reveal the back and ab tattoos, the denim shorts showing off the tight yoga asses, the tanned, brightly manicured feet traipsing around in flip-flops. The women were uniformly attractive but completely alien, like brightly colored plants that were likely poisonous.

Across the way, Meg could see the windows to some of the hotel rooms. On the third floor, two young women in underwear were frolicking around the room.

"Don't they know people can see them?" Meg asked him.

"I'm sure. They probably like it that way," Tristan said.

He watched her watching the girls. She tried to keep her facial expression neutral, but the truth was, she found the sight of the women slightly titillating. And he knew this, of course.

Meg wished she'd never admitted to him that she was attracted to women. She'd made this confession early in the relationship. She found his intense physicality, and his openness about sexuality, so thrilling. She felt she could tell him that she was attracted to other women and he would not judge her or be threatened by it. And she had been right: he was not threatened by it. In fact, he wanted to help her experience the one thing she had fantasized about, but never actually experienced.

"I don't understand why, if you're attracted to women, you've never acted on it," he'd said to her.

"It's not that simple," she'd said. "Life isn't a porn movie. Girls don't just walk around making out with one another."

He'd said he would help her "get a girl." He said her problem was that as an attractive woman, she had no idea how to "put it out there"—her job had always been to fend off guys hitting on her. She was uncomfortable doing the hitting on.

This was true, but irrelevant as far as she was concerned. Yes, she was attracted to women, but she'd made it this far in life without sleeping with one. And yet throughout their two-year relationship, when they were at a party or a club or a bar, he would gesture toward an attractive woman—one he knew was her type—and suggest they chat her up. Did Tristan know that she found the women attractive, or was he simply attracted to them himself? This question preoccupied her, and made her want to be with a girl less and less.

Meg watched the women in the window, wondering if they were getting dressed to go out, and where they would go. Then she turned her back on them and looked out at the city. They were just visiting L.A., as they did every so often. It was a beautiful spring night. She should have been happy, but she was overwhelmed by the distance she felt from him. Is this how it felt when a relationship was over?

"Do you want to go?" he asked. He knew she was detached, and it was bothering him. She could have reached for his hand as they walked back to the lobby, but she didn't.

Outside, they walked down Sunset toward the apartment where they were staying. She didn't want to go home for the night and just stew in the tension until they fell asleep, but what else was there to do?

A block down the street, they passed a building with no windows. The sign said BODY WORKS. Painted on the side of the building was a silhouette of a female nude.

"Do you want to go in?" he said.

"Okay," Meg said. She had never been to a strip club before. He wasn't a big strip-club guy, either. She wondered why he'd suggested it. Maybe he felt anything was better than the silence between them.

"It might be too early, but we can try it."

Inside, he paid the cover, and they were told since it was an all-nude club, there was no alcohol served.

A curved stage with half a dozen poles was in the far end of the room. A few guys were seated around the edge—a serious-looking Native American dude, and two shell-shocked looking tourists who had maybe wandered into the wrong place, and a stunt double for Bill Gates. The early bird crew. Loud metal played over the sound system.

"Sorry—this seems pretty bad," he said. He bought the mandatory two beverages for each of them.

"It's fine," Meg said, sipping her bottle of Perrier. She

wondered what the women would look like. She imagined them with blonde hair and big fake tits and lots of tattoos. She knew she would feel more uncomfortable than turned on, but she was grateful for the distraction.

There were no women on the stage.

"Maybe we should just leave," he said.

"It's fine," she repeated. And it was. What else did they have to do? Go back to the hotel and finish their stupid argument?

And then a woman walked out and stood at the pole directly in front of them. The first thing Meg thought was that she had a perfect body. Why this was shocking to her, she had no idea. She was, after all, at a strip club. But she hadn't expected the woman's body to be so beautiful. The long legs, yes, but her breasts were exquisitely shaped and proportionate to her body, not the cartoonish balloon breasts like the strippers on television shows. Her hair was long and dark. And the shoes! She wore black patent-leather platform heels, at least four inches high. They were shoes Meg would wear in another life, shoes that embodied a power and sexuality that Meg had experienced only in the most fleeting moments, and even those only recently, with Tristan.

Meg felt self-conscious. Tristan knew the woman was her type. Already, she could feel him watching for her reaction.

The woman wound her lithe body around the pole, and Meg watched her with fascination. She admired how the woman moved her body, how she commanded the room—how she owned it.

She jumped up on the pole and locked her legs around it, then arched her back until her hair hung down almost touching the floor. She swung around and jumped off. Men were throwing singles on the stage. Then she walked to the edge of the stage and they stuffed bills in her G-string. Meg couldn't take her eyes off of her. And then her boyfriend pressed money into her hand.

"Give it to her," he whispered in her ear. No, she couldn't.

But then the woman was stretched out on her back in front of Meg, her hair fanning over the edge of the stage and brushing Meg's thighs. From that prone position, the girl kicked her legs, then quickly turned around so her breasts were in Meg's face. Close enough for Meg to smell her bubble gum.

The bills felt damp in Meg's hand. When she reached out and put them in the girl's G-string, her movements were clumsy. Meg's head was buzzing, and she was thankful she hadn't had any alcohol.

And then, before she left the stage, the woman leaned over and said something to Tristan. Meg found this mildly curious, but thoughts were slipping in and out of her mind by that point, slippery fish escaping the net.

Meg was ready to leave.

Tristan leaned in to whisper to her, "She said if you want, you can go into a back room with her."

"Me?" Meg said.

"Yes, you."

"For what? Like, a lap dance or something?"

"Or something," he said.

"Are you serious?"

"Yeah. She said she likes girls."

Meg turned away. She looked at the stage. It was empty now.

"Okay," she said.

"You want to?"

"Yes," she said.

They stood up and Meg followed him to the back of the club, through a curtain, into a dark room with some tables and chairs. "I'm going to get more money," he said to her quietly. "I'll be right back. Are you okay?" He squeezed her arm.

"Yes," she said. That was all she seemed capable of saying. And then somehow the girl was there beside her.

"We don't have to do anything you don't want to do," she said sweetly. "I know sometimes guys like to watch, so if you don't want to do anything really I know how to fake it."

"It's okay. I'm fine. Really," Meg said. The girl reached out and stroked her hair. For the first time, Meg did not wonder about Tristan's motivation. She knew he was giving this experience to her.

When Tristan came back from the ATM, the girl led them to a small vestibule that was curtained off. Meg and Tristan sat next to each other on the ottoman that was essentially a long, padded bench. The girl stood in front of Meg and took off her top, leaving her wearing just a black G-string and the shiny, dramatic high heels.

The girl was tanned and toned and perfect. Meg knew she had to do something, but she didn't know what. She decided to just do what she wanted to do, which was to reach out and touch the girl's breasts. She was amazed by the feel of her soft and smooth skin that seemed to give off heat.

"Can she kiss you?" Tristan said.

"She can do whatever she wants," said the girl.

Meg leaned forward and kissed her. She touched the girl's hair and was amazed by its luxurious thickness. And that cherry bubble-gum smell! Was it perfume? Lotion?

The girl's mouth was soft, and it did feel different to Meg than kissing a guy. It was also strange to be kissing and touching someone who was being paid. But there was no hint that the girl was just doing a job—she was sweet, and encouraging, and kissed her as if she were having fun.

And yet Meg was overwhelmed. She didn't know what to do next. And then she knew she wanted the woman to go to Tristan.

Meg was surprised to hear the request come out of her mouth, because her intense jealousy was a hallmark of their relationship. But she wanted Tristan to experience this girl, to feel her skin and her hair and to know this odd experience.

The girl climbed onto Tristan's lap. She ground against him, and Tristan touched her breasts. Meg tried to read the expression on his face, but she couldn't. And then he looked at her, and when their eyes met, she felt a connection to him that was more intense that any she had ever felt. She loved him so much in that moment, it was as if all the baggage and tension in their relationship evaporated. She realized that she did not have to worry about him wanting other women. Even with this gorgeous creature naked in his lap, he was looking at Meg. And now she could easily read the expression on his face: it was love for her.

Tristan said something to the woman, but Meg couldn't hear.

"Lie down," he told Meg. She complied, shifting onto her back. The woman began unbuttoning Meg's blouse. Meg never wore a bra, and now the woman was looking at her bare breasts. Meg closed her eyes, and felt the girl's mouth on her nipples while at the same time, Tristan moved his hand under her skirt, his fingers inside her as the girl's tongue played with her breasts. The experience was so intense, Meg couldn't help but moan. The girl pressed her face close to hers.

"Sshh," she said, softly.

The girl kissed her, her hands now on her breasts while Tristan stroked Meg's pussy. He always knew just how to touch her, reaching a spot deep inside that no one ever had before. He was doing it then, moving in and out with practiced strokes, reaching that spot only to retreat, and then returning to the spot until she shuddered with an orgasm so intense, it took all her effort not to make a sound.

And then, the dark curtain rustled. The girl went to it, speaking to someone just outside. Nervously, Meg buttoned her shirt. She looked at Tristan, and he smiled at her.

The girl came back. Their time was up.

Meg and Tristan stepped out into the night, the sunset long over. He reached for her hand. As he held her, guiding her down the busy street toward their temporary home, she found it hard to believe that an hour ago she'd thought the relationship was ending. Now, for the first time, she knew it was not going to end—not that night, not ever.

BREAK

Cheryl B.

My ex-girlfriend Kate invited me over for dinner. The minute she opened the door I was reminded of what had attracted me to her from the beginning: the blue eyes, dark spiky hair, small sturdy body and the perfectly round bottom covered in baggy jeans. I wanted to turn her around and smack her ass, but we hadn't seen each other in over two months and had more pressing things to get over first.

After the awkward hello hug, we sat down at her kitchen table for the lasagna, which she had baked to perfection and served with a crisp salad and warm bread. I'd almost forgotten what a good cook she was. Almost forgotten that on our first date, Kate had described herself as a domestic butch. "I like to cook," she had said. "And I like to eat," I answered before pushing her head down on the bed.

When we were finished with the lasagna, we moved into the living room where we sat on separate parts of her sectional couch to watch the DVD. It doesn't matter what the movie was.

I found myself trying to figure out a way to smoothly move myself onto her section of the couch. Maybe if I stretched out far enough, I would touch her leg. I tried this several times, but couldn't completely work it.

The last time I sat on this couch with her, she lay across my knee as I smacked her fleshy cheeks with a paddle. I'd worked it into a good rhythm, moving from one red-welted cheek to another with an intensity that almost scared me.

"Baby, I don't think I can take any more," Kate cried.

"Oh, you're going to take it." I picked up the rhythm.

"It feels so good," she acquiesced.

"I bet it does." I continued smacking.

But that night I kept my distance as she didn't seem too interested in crossing over onto my area of the couch.

Following the movie, we stood in her doorway for the good-bye.

"It's late," I said, looking at the clock on the wall.

"What do you mean by that?" she asked cautiously.

I reached out and touched her hand—I couldn't help myself. When she touched me back, it was obvious we were both under the spell of the familiar.

"I mean it's past midnight," I offered.

"Does that mean you want to stay over?" Kate asked.

"Do you want me to?"

"If you want to."

"Are you sure?"

"Yeah, it's too late. The bus is weird now."

"I can sleep on the couch."

"You don't have to do that."

"Are you sure?"

"Yes."

Kate handed me my favorite red flannel pajamas. The ones

I'd always worn when I stayed over during our two-year relationship. They were soft and warm and as soon as they were in my hands, I realized how much I'd missed them. Or perhaps I'd just missed her. I went into the bathroom to change. Just a few months prior, I would have disrobed right in the middle of the living room, but since we were broken up I felt self-conscious. I was surprised that she had even kept the pajamas, and I was even more surprised to find my pink toothbrush waiting for me in her medicine cabinet in the same spot I had always kept it. But then her toothbrush was still in my cabinet too. I didn't want to throw it out. "Lesbian couples never really break up," someone said to me years ago, "they just find new ways to be codependent." I never thought that was true. I'm not one of those people who can be friends with my exes, so this was new territory for me.

Kate's new girl made her presence known in the bathroom as well. There was an unfamiliar hair product sitting out on the sink next to expensive loose powder. On the shelf above were two tacky hair accessories with long strands of blonde hair still attached. I picked up one of the barrettes and studied the specimen. I could tell by the way the hair caught the light that that other girl was a natural blonde. Kate always told me she didn't like blondes; she only liked brunettes, like me. My ex-boyfriend told me he didn't like women with large breasts, he only liked women with smaller chests, like me. You can imagine where that went when we broke up.

By the time I got ready, Kate was already in bed, tucked up to her chin, journal in hand. I didn't know what to expect. Was this really just a friendly sleepover? Were we going to get it on? Even worse, I didn't know what I wanted to have happen. I got into the bed and she stopped writing, ending the entry with an exaggerated flourish of her pen. She put the journal on her nightstand and I realized that I'd never seen her write in a journal before. Was this a new thing? *So much can happen in two months,* I thought as I ducked down under the covers.

She shut off the light and moved closer to me, placing her arm around my waist. I didn't know whether to burst out crying or kiss her desperately. Either way, the weight of our separation was apparent and we melted into each other as if nothing had happened, as if we'd never broken up.

I rolled on top of her and held down her arms.

"I'm your prisoner," Kate said playfully.

"Oh, yes you are." I reached over the side of her bed and felt around for her wrist restraints. They were still attached to the bed frame, one on each side. It was nice to see my girl hadn't lost her lust for pervery. I tuned her around, belly down, bottom up, and tightly fastened each wrist.

"Stick your pretty ass in the air," I whispered in her ear.

She did as I told her, pushing her ass out in exaggeration. I pulled her satin blindfold off the bedpost and fastened it around her head.

"Oh, no!" she cried.

I opened the bottom drawer of her nightstand, where she kept the supplies, and felt around for her riding crop. It was at the bottom. Did this mean she hadn't used it in a while? Was blondie not into spanking? I spread her knees farther apart and fastened each ankle in its restraint.

"Don't move," I told her and smacked her ass hard with my hand just to emphasize the seriousness of the situation.

"Yes," she answered.

"Yes, what?"

"Yes, Ma'am," she answered. This was all part of our game and I was ecstatic to hear that she hadn't forgotten the dialogue.

Then I picked up the riding crop, got off the bed and walked a few feet back to regard the situation; my little domestic butch prisoner was waving her ample ass in the air, just waiting for it. No one else had ever done this to me: turned me into such a dirty, foul-mouthed bitch with a bad attitude and a steady, sadistic hand. Before Kate, I was not particularly interested in much outside the typical fucking and sucking that had been part of my existence as a bisexual woman, but something about her brought out my femme top.

She was really begging for it now, wiggling her bottom in the air.

"You better smack my ass soon, or else," she implored, barely able to move any part of her body except her ass, which was thrusting wildly. I could see her pussy slick and glistening from behind.

"Or else what?" I laughed, my own juices bubbling over inside my panties. "What are you going to do to me? You're all tied up."

"I'll smack your ass," she said defiantly. She knew that was never going to happen.

"You're going to smack *my* ass?"

"Yes, I'm going to smack your ass if you don't start smacking mine. Please, please don't make me wait any longer."

I stepped closer to the bed. She whimpered in anticipation. I ran my implement across her cheeks, down her crack, and separated her soaking wet lips with the tip of the riding crop. She began to tremble all over, practically falling over on one side, her ass falling toward the bed.

"Get up. Put your ass back in the air," I said, lightly smacking her bottom with the palm of my hand.

"Yes, Ma'am!" she said. She was shaking, but she got back up and once again assumed the position.

I continued to play with her pussy lips and rub her clit with the riding crop. The black leather skated easily over the deep red folds of wet flesh. I wanted to reach down and taste her but managed to focus on the task at hand. I backed away, raised my arm over my head and brought the riding crop down on the flesh of her left buttcheek. She gasped then moaned.

I watched as the skin rose, forming a perfect red welt. I raised my arm even farther above and came down on the right side. I thought about the blonde, leaving her hair all over the place and staking her claim in the bathroom. I imagined her paws all over Kate. The bitch had probably even worn my pajamas! My favorite pajamas! I bore down on Kate's ass with a fierce velocity. With each break on her ass, I thought about "The Break" we had taken in our relationship. What a brilliant idea that was! "Breaks" never work out, they're just ways to belabor the "Breaking Up" process, throw another wrench into the already gut-wrenching mix, which then just spins around and hits you in the head. I noticed a long blonde hair on the sheet by Kate's knee and I was filled with an incredible sadness.

I thought about the guy I'd been with since "The Break"—as bland as a bowl of vanilla ice cream and even less satisfying. No one will ever bring out *his* inner pervert. He has no inner pervert. Some people are just like that, and you have to accept it. But I keep going back because I don't know what else to do. It's hard to meet people in this city, and I've never been one to be alone.

I'd heard from a good friend that Kate was crazy about the blonde, and as I stood there lovingly beating her ass to a fuchsia-tinted pulp, I somehow knew that no matter how much we wanted each other that night, we would never be together again.

When Kate yelled for me to stop, I collapsed on top of her, both of us crying like we did when we first fell in love. Her ass was warm against the front of my flannel pajamas, and we both fell facedown on a bed that could no longer contain us.

IN THE MIRROR

Valerie Alexander

I was putting my pearls on for the rehearsal dinner when my husband's thoughts turned to Hanna. He was sitting on the edge of the hotel bed, with that thoughtful expression on his chiseled face that made him look introspective. It was the face he made when he was attracted to someone new. Which meant he wasn't thinking about Toby, his boyfriend back home. And I knew, because he was my soul mate and erotic twin, that it wasn't the bellhop who'd brought up our bags, or one of the groomsmen in the wedding we were attending tomorrow. He was thinking about my girlfriend, Hanna.

They'd met last summer when I started dating her, but they hadn't spent any real time together before she returned to art school. But now we were in her city, and she had picked us up today at the airport. She'd given a brief tour along the way to the hotel and Will had watched her face with a suspicious, slightly amazed expression, like he'd never seen her before. We always got to know each other's lovers; it was part of our agreement and a way of signaling to them that there would be no shifting priorities or betrayals. Just like when he started sleeping with Toby two months ago, and we had him over for dinner. What wasn't part of our official agreement was that we only slept with our own gender, but somehow it had worked out that way. None of the men who hit on me ever compared to my perfect husband. Or maybe it was that I enjoyed a chase, and women were always so much more elusive and therefore all the more alluring for the chance to experience that aching, tantalizing arc from falling for a woman to the first time I held her naked in my arms.

Hanna, of course, was the sweetest ache of all, my doe-eyed little art student who looked so serious and dedicated while painting yet fucked with a feverish, half-sobbing passion that amazed and besotted me every time. People thought she was pretty but they rarely twigged to her carnal potential; watching my husband in the mirror now, I suspected he had.

"Are they serving lamb tonight?" I asked. "I think that's what my cousin said."

"Lamb?" He stirred from his reverie. My sweet husband, so romantic and generous with boys, never as calculating or intuitive as me, his wife. It was why I loved him. "I don't know. We'll get you something later if there's nothing you can eat." Then, because he never knew when he was being obvious: "Hanna knows the area, Jamie. She'll know where to go."

"I know. I just don't want to offend anyone by not eating the dinner." This was my cousin's wedding we were attending. She knew I was a vegetarian but tonight would mainly be her fiancé's family and they were conservative.

I turned before the mirror each way, testing the fall of my dark purple dress, the shimmer of my recently highlighted hair. Will hugged me from behind. "You look beautiful," he said, but he always said that. I rubbed my hand against his jaw and thought that I was the lucky one, with a handsome husband so deep in adoration of me, so mesmerized by the same sexual multiverse that mesmerized me. We understood each other perfectly.

The rehearsal dinner was quiet and strained. Both tonight's dinner and the wedding tomorrow were being held in a five-star hotel that was apparently off season. Will and I had taken to calling it the Overlook from *The Shining*, because it was the dead of winter and the huge lobby stayed ominously empty. "It'll pick up tomorrow," Will murmured to me over dinner (which was indeed a choice of lamb or salmon). Almost everyone attending the rehearsal dinner was from my cousin's fiancé's family, and they were all keen to know our Nice Young Couple story: how we met, where we worked, how long we'd been married. We gave answers that edited out the dank hustler bar we'd met in and smiled when assured our future children would be gorgeous.

I picked at my risotto, the disturbance of a strange environment shifting into a shaky restlessness for sex. I was in Hanna's city. She was coming to the hotel tonight for a drink, but tomorrow after the wedding was over, we were going to have a real date in her bed. An acute pining for her body spread through me now. Tonight, I decided, would not be just a drink. We would go off for a quickie in some distant parking lot, for just long enough to feel her warm pillowy body against mine.

I discreetly checked my phone. ELEVEN O'CLOCK, her text message said. I showed it to Will, about to say *I might need a little private time with her later, is that okay?* But a false and careful neutrality arranged itself on his face.

"Cool," he said. "This will be fun."

He definitely had a crush on her. That changed things.

After the rehearsal dinner, we changed upstairs. There was

a sense of emancipation, of escaping the grown-ups' table to transform into the nocturnal deviants we really were. Despite the winter night outside, Will only wore an old T-shirt. I told myself he wasn't really trying to look straight for Hanna. I took off my pearls, though I had a yen to see her wear them naked, and changed into a tight black sweater and jeans. My makeup was still holding up, and so was my hair. We went down to the bar and had a drink.

Someone had to say it. "What's wrong with us tonight?" I asked.

Will looked at his hands like a shy schoolboy. It was hard to tell if he felt guilty, falling for my lover, or if he was disconcerted because it was a girl.

Then Hanna came in, her grin lighting up the bar darkness. She was so wholesome-looking in her winter jacket and jeans, her dark hair bouncing around her shoulders like a shampoo commercial. My stomach flip-flopped like always and then she was on me, hugging me tight and crying, "Hi," in that exuberant way of hers.

I had to force myself to let go of her. God, I was clingy tonight. She sat on my lap for just a moment, the wonderful weight of her ass crushing me—I had a specific appreciation for feeling the heft of her spread out on top of me in bed—and complimented my hair, then rose again. She barely glanced at Will. Then I realized she was looking at someone else.

He came loping through the bar with a moody face, all floppy brown hair and dangling car keys. He was her age, from her art school, no doubt, and probably a boyfriend. He was too adorable not to be. I wondered if he knew she and I were going to fuck each other raw tomorrow night.

"Will, Jamie, this is Connor," she said. Introductions all around. Hanna seemed excited, high on the energy of the night.

It electrified the bar like an antidote to the half-empty hotel and frozen landscape outside. "He and his roommates are having a party tonight. Do you guys want to go?"

I think Will and I both felt acutely thirty-two at that moment. Not that we were old, not that we didn't go to parties, but a college party is a specific milieu we'd left behind long ago.

But alcohol and crashing music loud enough to drown in signaled the antidote to our woes. "Sure," we said together.

Off we went into the night. If we felt old in the bar, Connor's ancient car with its rattling struts and his reckless speeding over the ice made us hold hands in the backseat. Hanna sat up front and talked animatedly about her multimedia installation project. She was much more extroverted here on her home turf, I noticed. Back home, she'd been my shy girl. I shifted my study to Connor: pretty lips, flawless skin, little to no awareness of his fuck puppy appeal. And that mop of hair, good god, my fingers ached to stroll through it like the gardens of Versailles.

I never fantasized about Hanna with others, the way I did with Will. It was enough just to think about her kneeling naked at my feet with that mischievous yet obedient look. Or remember pushing her over the sofa with her skirt up and her ripe ass and pussy on display for the plundering. But watching her and Connor fuck was suddenly topping my erotic wish list.

They debated the appearance tonight of a band they knew. I noted that he listened to her and accepted her opinions and that they knew how to make each other laugh. How long had they been dating? I glanced at my husband to see which of them he was checking out. But Will was looking at me.

"And we're here." Connor pulled up to the curb on a long dark street of what looked like abandoned buildings.

It was a loft party. We climbed a few dozen stairs to enter a red-lit darkness thick with the smell of weed, spilled beer and various chemical art supplies. It was overheated and not terribly loud: there was no band, but an old Smiths album on a turntable, scratchily playing through giant amps. Connor and Will took our coats and I took advantage of their absence by pulling Hanna into a semiprivate alcove.

Her sweet mouth covered mine and her hands roamed over me with almost rapacious greed. "I miss you," she whispered into my mouth. "I've really, really needed you," and I couldn't even answer her back because I hungered for her entire body so badly at that instant. I undid her jeans and she fell back against the wall as I tugged them with her underwear down far enough to finger her. Hanna loved being taken without preamble, no consideration or foreplay needed, and she spread her legs as wide as her tangled jeans allowed. Her pussy felt incredibly hot and quivery around my fingers as I diddled her. Then I understood her half-closed eyes were on someone else.

I looked over my shoulder to find Will watching us. "Sorry," he said and vanished.

Hanna was already coming on my hand. "Don't stop," she said and draped herself around me, squeezing me tight as she finished. But that was a very fast come even for her, and I knew she'd gotten off on being watched. Or on Will watching, specifically.

She slid her hands up my sweater. "I've been *craving* you," she said, squeezing my breasts. "I can't wait for tomorrow night."

Tomorrow seemed a year away. "Does your boyfriend understand?"

"Yeah, he knows. I mean, it's all new to him; he's very sheltered. But I explained things."

I wondered if sheltered Connor was straight. I wondered how he fucked her. I pulled up her jeans and we kissed for the first time. She was still holding me and melting all of my tensions when there was a scuffle behind us and Connor apologized, then scooted away.

"Apparently we're wanted." I kissed her again, remembering her last visit, when we'd finished fucking for the fifth time around daybreak but were too wired to sleep. We couldn't stop kissing and playing with each other's fingers, giddy with the adolescent thrill of being two naked girls in a bed together. "Come on."

We joined the party. A new album was on the turntable, something equally morose. So much for the artists' bacchanalia Will and I expected. There seemed to be only beer available, which I didn't drink. More people walked in with bagged bottles, and we crowded onto a ripped loveseat together, Will, then me, then Hanna on Connor's lap. Most of the lights were off and the glow of electric space heaters and the music's drone were calming me into an easier tranquility. Hanna was talking about her project again. Connor's dark eyes were on me, speculative and assessing. I wasn't his enemy, but he wasn't sure how to categorize me. The small loveseat forced his thigh against mine and though I could have moved onto Will's lap, I stayed in the middle, enjoying the charge from their bodies bracketing mine.

Will caressed the back of my neck. "He's cute."

"The kid?" That was feigned ignorance and he knew it. "I'm here for Hanna."

"He can't take his eyes off you. I don't mind."

Of course he didn't, because that paved his path to Hanna. "Then you take him."

"He's obviously straight, Jamie."

A live wire was stirring in my pussy, a blur of desire and heat. I wanted all three of them on top of me, fucking me and servicing me like the lazy bottom I so rarely was, a ménage of Hanna's breasts and Will's hands and ridiculously, Connor's hair. I almost always knew the right etiquette, the right moves. But tonight I felt unmoored from all of our usual codes and lost in what felt like irreconcilable longings.

Another guy plunked himself on the loveseat arm, shoving us even closer together. Hanna got up to hug a girl by the keg. I looked at Will. He looked the most out of place here, too pretty, his short brown hair in too trendy a cut. I could still look young and casually slutty in the right light. Or rather, the right dark.

"You want a beer?" he asked. "When in Rome..."

"Sure. Hit the keg for me." We laughed at our relative oldness because the truth was, it made us feel like a special brand of visitor here, an incubus and succubus team.

He swam off into hazy dark. Connor's friend was gone and I looked at Connor to see if I should move over and break this tacit closeness between us. He was looking at me with open hunger. I looked him over, too: he was the canvas my beautiful girl was spreading herself on these days and I wanted to know her nightly litany. His chest, his thighs, his fresh young come and silky hair. Everything.

"You're not what I was expecting," he said.

Meaning the older predatory couple, "swingers," insert tacky stereotype here. "I wasn't expecting you at all."

The album had played to the end. A rhythmic scratchiness repeated over and over without anyone noticing. Which made me notice that Will hadn't come back with my beer and Hanna hadn't come back from her friend.

Sometimes when you're in the dark at a party with someone, there's a moment when words end and the two of you unite in a private and momentary space. When your minds meet in an intention that's based on an illusion, but at that moment feels shared and real. I slid into Connor's lap and we started kissing. I put my hands in that bouquet of soft brown hair and let the musty-smelling dark envelop us, the smell of beer, the ripped couch beneath us. On a different night, I would have eaten him whole. But tonight I slid off his lap and led him to the back of the loft.

They were on a futon covered with coats. I held my breath in anticipation of watching my husband fuck my girlfriend, but they weren't touching. Hanna was naked and cross-legged like a Tantric goddess, the glow of a corner space heater turning her skin a reddish-gold. Her face was serious in a familiar expression, her hand moving between her legs. Will was on his knees, jeans pushed down as he stroked his cock and watched her finger herself.

My heart gave an odd thump as I watched this tableau of exhibitionism and twisted fidelity. Connor stepped up behind me, pressing his erection into my ass. I let him undress me as if he were my page and then I walked naked to Hanna who looked up at me with a loving smile.

Her mouth opened in an invitation to use her tongue. Instead I crawled on top of her, pushing her down into the coats and sinking into her heavenly softness. I let my mouth melt over hers, her tongue sweet as honey as my fingers relearned every curve of her body. She knew my preference for feeling her sprawl on top of me, and so she carefully rolled me onto my back. Gripping my forearms, she rubbed herself all over me, burying my face in her voluptuous breasts and kissing my throat. She was already slightly damp with sweat, and her thighs clung to mine, our stomachs dragging together, as she slowly moved down my body. She opened my legs like she was opening a present, her thumbs in the hollows of my thighs. A thousand tiny shivers ran around my skin in anticipation. They burst into fireworks as her soft pillowy tits settled on my pussy. This was my favorite way to come with her, my favorite way to remember her, the very best way for her to pay homage to my smitten, lovestruck worship of her.

Moving her dark hair out of her face, she began to rub her nipple on my clit. I groaned, surrendering to that divine sensation only she could provide. Will and Connor were watching her, too, my young naked goddess grinning as she lifted up her breasts and shook them before burying my cunt in their softness again.

"Fuck me," I begged, straining my legs open wider. "Hanna, please." So many girls in my past would have fainted to hear me beg anyone, but with her it was electrifying. She bit my thighs, her tits sliding around my wetness. With shameless urgency, I trapped her in my legs. Then I humped her ruthlessly, grinding against her nipples as a searing heat flooded my pussy and a throbbing storm of an orgasm rolled through me.

I dropped my head and tried to catch my breath. She crawled up on top of me. The electric space heater's orange coils were illuminating the dark room, and the movement of a shadow prodded me to look over at Will and Connor. Will was still kneeling on the futon, fully naked now, his hard thighs flexed and spread as he fisted his own cock. And in one of the best surprises of the night, Connor stood naked in front of him, his dick buried balls-deep in my husband's mouth.

Oh, my voyeuristic joy. Watching my husband suck off another man was one of my secret pleasures, and all too rarely indulged. I knew a straight college boy's dick was one of his secret thrills, and the stunned, dizzy look on Connor's face told me Will was unleashing all of his oral tricks on him now. I was torn between succumbing to the visual spell of Hanna's face over mine like a star or the always wondrous sight of my husband coming all over another man's body. As if reading my mind, Will's fist began to fly faster and his orgasm erupted in pearly spurts that clung to Connor's thighs.

Hanna lowered her nipples onto my tongue to be sucked clean. "I really have missed you," she whispered into my ear. Her wet body felt deliciously intense on top of mine. She kissed me again, her tongue parting my lips, and together we opened our legs. In a practiced friction, we began to grind against each other, working each other's clits into a delirious incandescence.

Hanna buried her face in my hair, moaning helplessly. Her cunt felt so wet and hot on mine that I was close to coming again. A long groan filled the room and I looked over to see Connor pumping his orgasm into my husband's mouth, hips working furiously. But Hanna was oblivious to him, clawing me and almost sobbing as she pushed her clit into me with all her might. With a broken cry, she reared up on both elbows and came in a small warm gush on my pussy.

We rolled apart. The room was hot and thick with the smell of sex and all of us were breathing hard. Hanna rolled onto her back, looking at Will, then me. I nodded and she spread her legs in an obvious invitation.

Will froze. "Go on," I said. "Please."

He took a long breath, then crawled between her legs. My entire body was taut with curiosity and excitement. Hanna reclined on the coats like an odalisque, playing with herself as Will stroked his cock hard again.

He mounted her with almost comical caution. She threw her legs open with immediate abandon and pinched her nipples, but he bit his lip with restraint as he slowly pushed his cock inside her. I knew he was savoring the novel sensation of his first new pussy since he married me. Memories of her heat and tightness flooded my mind as he gradually worked into a faster rhythm. Hanna was going off like a bomb beneath him, writhing and yowling like a cat in heat.

Will was still spearing in and out of her with a rigid jaw. I didn't know if it was because I was watching or because he was trying to hold back a red-hot eruption, but I took my place behind him, sliding my fingers into his ass and countering his every thrust.

He groaned. His whole body shivered in a way that only happened when his balls were tight and he was on the verge of rocketing into space on a cosmic orgasm. He fucked Hanna harder, faster now, his hips a blur of rhythm and dexterity. Connor was between my legs, licking and fingering my pussy, but I barely felt it, so focused was I on Will and Hanna's intensely feverish faces. Hanna let out a raw cry of surprised joy, and Will's asshole closed around my fingers as he began to come with one final, shuddering moan. I quietly pushed Connor away from my clit and brought myself off in vicarious bliss.

The ice-rimmed windows were turning blue with winter dawn. The dim light brought into focus the coats we had just fucked on, the student paintings on the walls. I scuttled back from the three of them so I could compose a memory: their wet rumpled hair and shadowed faces, the tangle of limbs and curves like a Roman orgy. It could have been a beautiful mirage, everything I wanted but was afraid to ask for, but it was real. It was my real life.

Back in the hotel, Will and I took a hot bath, then slept for three hours. Dressing for the wedding later that day, my mind was a languorous, satisfied emptiness. As I put on my pearls again, I wondered what kind of marriage my cousin would have and what she and her husband would find together.

Will came up behind me, so handsome and perfectly coiffed that he could have been the groom figure on top of a wedding cake. "You look beautiful."

"So do you."

Something happens when your eyes meet in the mirror. A sense of unity, an ineffable pact that verges on self-congratulation. It's like a spell, the way some knowledge can only appear in a reflection.

Will clasped my pearls and ran his fingers across my nape. "It's always going to be like this," he said. "We're always going to be exceptional."

"Do you think so?" We looked at each other a moment more. Then I turned and kissed him and we went down to the wedding.

GLITTER IN
THE GUTTER

Giselle Renarde

I wouldn't say that I *stormed* into Hina's office—*marched* was more like it. When she didn't react, I just came right out and asked, "What happened to Connor? We haven't been on the schedule together since..." I stopped myself before I could say, "Since that time he dressed like a woman and took me out for Thai food and we had sex in his hatchback in the underground parking lot." There were only so many times a story like that should be told among coworkers.

Hina looked up at me with those big dairy-cow eyes and my knees went weak. Sure, I was in love with Connor, but I'd had a crush on Hina from the day she hired me. There was something about that dark hair, honey-brown skin and thick lashes I found inexorably exotic, even after I found out she'd grown up in Mississauga just like the rest of us.

"Dotschy..." She set aside the timesheets she'd been signing and shot me a sad smile. "You can't work all your shifts together, you two. You'll distract each other."

"No, we won't." I felt like a kid, and a whiny one at that. "It's just...he isn't returning my phone calls. I don't know what happened."

Hina's gaze flitted about the room like a frightened bird. She shuffled her papers without looking at them. "I don't know..." she echoed.

That's how I knew there was something to know. "What did he say to you?"

"Nothing," she stammered.

"Tell me what you know, Hina." I couldn't seem to prevent the rising irritation in my voice. I liked Hina, but I was just so desperate to find out why Connor wasn't speaking to me.

"You have to ask him," she said.

My hands formed themselves into fists, fingernails digging into flesh. "He won't take my calls!"

Hina let out a huffing breath and relented. "Connor says you're a bad influence."

I would have been taken aback if I understood for a moment what that might mean. "A bad influence on who?"

"On him." Hina's voice was Lilliputian as she chipped crimson polish from her ragged nails. "Look, you need to have this conversation between yourselves. It's too weird, being in the middle of it. I'm supposed to be your boss, for goodness' sake."

Really, I couldn't think what to say. In what world was I a bad influence on anybody? I was a good person, always arrived to work on time and neatly dressed. I ate healthy foods and gave money to charity and never played my music so loud it would bug the neighbors. How could Connor, the quirky, semi-closeted trans-curious cross-dresser I'd fallen head over heels for, think I was a bad person? What had I done to give him that idea?

The fact that he'd requested shifts that didn't overlap with mine made it difficult to get a conversation in. When I stuck

around the convention center one evening to see him, he just
plain ignored me; said he had work to do, no time to talk. His
absence was something I felt deep in my heart, like a stabbing
pain, but I couldn't give up on him. Connor meant the world
to me.

"What do you want?" he asked, when I knocked at his front
door. The convention center was closed for Victoria Day, the
one holiday Monday I always seemed to forget existed until it
arrived, so we both had time off.

"Connor!" I propped the door open when he tried to shut
it in my face. Forcing my way inside, I tripped over cushiony
garbage bags in the front entrance. "What the hell is all this?
Are you moving?"

"Somebody's moving," he said in a whispered growl. He was
already halfway up the stairs and I climbed over garbage bags
to follow. "Somebody's moving out of my life for good. Enough
is enough."

For a moment, I thought he meant me and my heart plunged
into my colon, burning. When I arrived at the top of the stairs
and looked beyond his bedroom's open door, I understood what
he meant. "Charlotte?" I asked, despite my certainty.

"Charlotte isn't real." He was tearing skirts and dresses from
the closet and heaving them into yet another green garbage bag,
sweat breaking across his brow. "I'm a man. What the hell am I
doing with all this shit?"

Watching this spectacle, I felt like a child. I had no idea how
to console him, what to say. All I could think about was the
accusation he'd made, the thing he'd said to Hina: I was a bad
influence. How?

"It looks nice on you," I said, perched at the top of his pink-
carpeted staircase. There was a sort of violence in Connor
that kept me out of his bedroom in that moment, although it

appeared self-directed. "I like Charlotte. I love her, actually. You can't just throw her away."

Connor turned to me then, like he was seeing me for the first time. His expression seemed composed, but that scared me too. "It's your voice in my head, you know." He opened a dresser drawer and took out the baby-pink cardigan he'd worn on our first date, holding it up to take a good long look at it. "It's your voice I hear saying: Charlotte, you're beautiful. Charlotte, you're stunning."

"You *are* beautiful," I'd just started to say, when Connor took the pink cardigan in hand and tried tearing it along the seam. Before I could think, I was bounding into the bedroom and over the garbage bag. "Stop it!" I shouted with all the pain it caused me to observe this ordeal. It hurt like hell, all this, like he was destroying me in the process. I grabbed the cardigan by one sleeve and pulled, trying to release it from his grip. Somehow, I ending up standing on his bed, trying to avoid hitting my head against the still blades of the ceiling fan. "What are you doing? Are you crazy?"

"Yes!" Connor let go of the cardigan and I tumbled down on his mattress, bouncing on yet another stack of clothing. It was only then I fully saw the pained expression on his face, like he was desperately holding back tears. He sunk like a defeated thing at the foot of the bed, and although there was an entire expanse of mattress between us, I felt a renewed closeness.

"Connor," I asked, "what's going on? Why don't you want to be with me anymore? And why are you getting rid of all your Charlotte clothes?"

He looked across the bed at me, a gaze so penetrating I had to break it and stare at the watercolor violets hanging in the hall. "Because I was wrong," he finally said, and this brought me back to his face, with its three-day beard and manicured eyebrows. "There is no Charlotte, only Connor. No more dressing up. I was sick to do that in the first place."

The voice was Connor's, but those were somebody else's words.

"What are you talking about?" I crawled across the bed on my hands and knees, leaving the pink cardigan at a safe distance. When I reached Connor, I cuddled into the generous expanse of his lap and hooked my chin around his shoulder, hugging the curvy body that was my mother and my father, and so very much more.

"I have to stop," he said. "I've already taken a full carload to the Sally Ann."

"Don't give to them," I replied without thinking. "They believe that queer people don't deserve salvation. They're really anti-gay." And then the complexity of what he'd just told me began to sink in, and I leaned back so I could look into his eyes. "Why are you giving all your clothes away?"

He blinked and looked quickly down at my fingers as they petted his beard. "Don't do that." He brushed my hand away, and then brushed me away, tripping over the garbage bag on his way to the bathroom. "I hate this. I need to shave."

I followed like a little ghost, perching on the toilet lid to watch him smother his cheeks in shaving cream. I didn't want to say anything shocking in case the controversy made him slip and cut his throat, but I had to ask, "What did I do?" I didn't mean about touching his stubble, but I think he knew that.

"You encouraged me," he replied.

"Yeah, so?"

"So..." Connor swished his razor around and then tapped it on the side of the sink. Feeling his cheek for stubbly spots, he shaved a few patches again. "It wasn't right, what I was doing. All those bags of clothes and, god, the makeup and shoes and purses and scarves and on and on...what kind of a man spends half his paycheck on women's clothing?"

"Even if they are for a woman?" I asked, knowing it wouldn't do a bit of good.

Connor met my gaze in the mirror as I crept in behind him. There were diamonds buried so deep in those eyes I could hardly even see them. But I knew they were there.

"You know I'm not a woman," he said, with such scorn in his voice I felt smaller than ever. "Or didn't you notice, when you were fucking me, that I have a cock?"

"There's no need to be crass." I was sounding dangerously like my mother now. "Anyway, you're the one who always said gender's between your ears, not between your legs. Why are you being so mean to me? I only ever supported you."

Pressing a hot towel to his face, he said, "Maybe I don't need support. Maybe what I need is to smarten up."

When he stormed out, I backed away and let him pass unhindered, but I followed him into the bedroom. I wasn't about to give up now. As I stood in the doorway, Connor picked up drugstore perfumes from the vanity and tossed them into the garbage bag one after another. Jewelry, too—junky stuff, but even so, it was hard to watch a person discard things with such malice.

"Did you know I used to be married?" he asked without looking at me.

It seemed like such a casual question, the way he asked it, but of course it wasn't. I was acting, too, when I pretended not to be shocked. "You never mentioned it, no."

"I'll give you one guess what brought that to an end." Connor tossed a tangled strand of pearls in with the rest and then collapsed on the bed, one arm strewn across his forehead, legs crossed at the ankles. He reminded me of Blanche DuBois, except that he was wearing black jeans and a strikingly blue button-down shirt. A satin gown would have suited him better, actually.

"I'm sorry," I said, not the least bit surprised when my voice faltered. It seemed strange that he hadn't mentioned a marriage before, and although I was curious I hoped he wouldn't say anything more on the subject. I didn't want to think about Connor with anyone but me.

"She went back out west when she made *the discovery*. I never brought her into that world. I tried to hide it, but wives, you know, they dig, dig, dig. Gotta know every little move you make. She called me all sorts of things when she found the clothes. I had a suitcase, kept it locked down in the basement, like it was a part of me, just hidden away." Connor didn't move from the bed, and I stood in the doorway wishing I didn't have to listen, but knowing love had to be endlessly receptive—that was its nature. "Moved in with her parents in Fort McMurray, and I dragged that suitcase down to the Sally Ann, tossed it in the donations Dumpster. Said never again. She was pregnant, you know, when she left."

I wanted to blend into the wallpaper, hide from this knowledge, but I heard myself asking, "When was this?"

"Almost six years."

"You have an almost-six-year-old?" I didn't mean to speak, but the words spilled out of me.

And then Connor said, "No," and everything inside of me went quiet. "Baby died. She blamed me. She blamed...all this."

My feet surprised me by carrying my body across the room and onto the bed. I tossed a pile of clothes to the floor so I could snuggle in next to Connor. Wrapping my arm around his middle, I lay my head down on his chest and assured him, "It's not your fault."

"Of course it is."

"It isn't." I hugged him as hard as I could, digging my face into the pillow of his being. I loved the curves he called fat. I loved the sweet arc of his belly and the man-boobs whose growth he readily encouraged with herbal supplements.

All I could think to do in that moment, the only thing that might make him feel better, was to open up his shirt and suckle those funny little breasts that swept upward like cones and peaked in silky nipples. I licked that soft pink flesh up and down with the tip of my tongue. When I felt his hand in my hair, I knew everything would be all right. A dainty moan escaped his lips when my licks turned to sucks, and I pressed his fleshy tits together to alternate between them.

"Dotschy," he whispered, his voice light as meringue, "please don't stop."

I didn't even pause to say, "I won't." I let my words vibrate against his nipples as I teased that precious flesh.

The idea of Connor being married, of another woman having done this to him, popped into my mind, and I pushed it away—pushed it hard. Is this how Connor had felt when I used to mention my ex? He'd never let on.

"I love you," I murmured into his flesh. I'm sure he recognized the sentiment, if not the muddled words. He pressed my head flush to his chest with one hand while the other struggled with the button and the zipper on his jeans. My hand followed his, twining with his fingers, pressing them away so I could do it on my own. When his fly was undone, I caught a hint of pink lace and broke my hold on Connor's breast to get a closer look.

"Oh." There was a sudden blush to his voice. "Well, the Sally Ann doesn't take panties and it would be such a shame to toss them out. This pair alone cost me twenty-five dollars. There's a matching camisole in the top drawer, there."

I slid from the bed and opened that treasure trove of a dresser drawer. Connor had the most beautiful underwear, all silk and satin, or lace and mesh. Panties with ruffles and ribbons, intricate trims. Nothing like my generic cotton. The matching pink lace camisole sat on top of a pile of silk slips and more matronly bras. When I turned around, Connor's clothes were on the floor. He sat propped up on both hands in a classic pinup pose, wearing only a pair of pink lace panties. His chest was shaved hairless, and when he raised his arms to let me dress him, I saw that his underarms were shaved, too. That made me want to lick them, for some reason, and so I did.

"What are you doing?" Connor laughed as he adjusted the pretty lace cami. Even when he'd put his arms back down, I crawled into his lap and licked the slit there with such persistence he laughed even harder. "Good thing I didn't put on deodorant this morning."

"Mmm-hmmm!" I straddled him, all hunched over so I could lap at the salty sweetness of his underarm. If only I'd stripped out of this sundress I'd worn just to please him, but it was easy enough to pull up on the hem until the gusset of my bright yellow undies met the thick heat buried inside Connor's pink lace. Until my pussy, shaved bare in preparation for this possibility, met Connor's hard shaft, I didn't realize how wet I'd become. Kissing his perfect pink lips, I writhed against his cock, letting its length rub my clit in easy, gentle strokes.

As we hummed mutual approval into each other's mouths, tongues swirling and mingling like tender serpents, Connor's loving hands descended my back. I wore dresses very rarely, but it felt wonderful to be touched inside that tight, light binding of cotton, to sense his fingers toying with the corset ties in back. I touched him, too, while we kissed. My fingers played along his bare arms, tickling his elbow-pits before traipsing down his sides. When he leaned back, I leaned forward, amazed we could derive such satisfaction in expressing our passions as tenderly as this.

If I'd pulled my skirt up all the way past my waist, I could have shown Connor the words TIGHT SPOT splashed across my panties in curlicue lettering. But he already knew that. He'd been there before. He clung to my waist as I lay on top of him, as though I'd attempt some escape, and I managed to lock my feet around his legs, which gave me better leverage in grinding my hips down hard against his. I could feel my wetness soaking through cotton, and probably through lace, as I traced tight circles around his cockhead with my clit. "That feels so good," I whispered against his lips.

I was surprised when he said, "Give me more."

Reaching between us, he freed his cock from its dainty prison, and the heat against my belly was astounding. He pushed and pulled at my panties, whatever it would take to get them off of me, and for a moment I wondered if it was Connor who'd said he'd had a vasectomy, or if I was confusing him with my ex. They both had, maybe? I could have just asked, but in the moment I was pretty sure he'd told me so. Was it because of the baby who'd died, I wondered? He wouldn't let that happen again, right? Or was I just making up excuses not to break this bond? I wanted him inside of me more than I wanted anything else in the world, except Connor's happiness, and what could make him happier than this?

I couldn't get my panties off without abandoning this frog-legged spread across Connor's body, so I pulled them to the side and let my bare lips kiss the solid length of his cock. My wetness trailed across his smooth flesh, and he shuddered beneath me, causing me to tremble in sympathy. His cock felt almost unbearably hot against my pussy, and it seemed the only remedy would be to take him inside. My hand struggled between our two bodies, but I found him, grasped him by the root and held him steady as I positioned his cockhead against my tremulous slit.

Connor whimpered when I sloped my body down, arching my back wildly so my hard nipples would poke out the top of my sundress. At first sight of them, Connor leaned forward to take one between his teeth. I moaned as he flicked it with the tip of his tongue, teasing me, and I teased him back by keeping the fullness of his cockhead at the entrance to my slit so long the waiting pained me. Finally, when Connor sucked my nipple fully into his mouth, I took his cock fully into my cunt, and we groaned in unison. I felt his voice reverberating in me, like that lilting timbre was intimately related to the hard thing throbbing inside my pussy.

We moved together, then, though my mobility vastly surpassed his. I ground my clit into the silken thicket of his pubic hair, grunting like a beast as Connor devoured my breasts. His cock had scarcely left the lace of his panties to enter my slit, and his balls were still trapped beneath the elastic. If I reached behind and around my ass, I could just barely scrape those bundled orbs with my fingernails, but that pressure seemed to be enough. Connor bucked up from underneath me, filling me so full of cock it would have panged at the peak of me if I hadn't been so aroused. There was no room left for anything but orgasm, and when I came hard, still grinding my clit against amber curls, he came too, shuddering, panting, uttering every sort of sweetness. I was groaning, grunting, animalistic, but Connor's voice was like wind chimes. Of course I couldn't tell him who to be, but I knew, at times, he was my woman.

I rested on top of him, like a kitten napping in the sun, his spent cock inside me, his heavy hands on my back. "I'm sorry about the baby," I said when I was too far gone to care about my pride. "I'm sorry about your wife, too. She was wrong, you know."

"I know." Connor sighed in that lovely feminine way of his. "It's just...it gets me down at times, feeling trapped between one thing and the other, and I tell myself to be a man. That's the simple solution. Stop with the dressing. Get rid of the clothes. Be a man."

"Are you a man?" I asked, playing, but curious what his answer would be.

Growling, laughing, Connor rolled me over so his weight bore down on mine. "Sometimes I am." He nuzzled my neck, making me giggle despite myself. "And sometimes I'm not. Sometimes I'm everything at once—and you get that. That's why you're dangerous."

Pinned beneath his heavy body, I gasped, "That's what makes me a bad influence?"

"Bad, bad, bad!" he scolded, tickling my armpits. At least he wasn't licking them. His cock had slipped from me in the mock-struggle, and he tucked it back into his underwear when he sat up to look at me. Clean-shaven and dressed in that lovely pink lace, he looked so beautiful I almost cried. "Ever been Dumpster diving?"

I sat up, too, leaning back against the headboard and knowing just what he meant. "Would you believe I have?"

"Liar!" Connor had the kind of teasing smile that could light up a room. "Have you really?"

I nodded. "When I was in high school, my friend Erika's mother was a little...unbalanced, I guess? Like, protective and possessive and all that. When Erika said she was going to the States for university—college, I guess they call it there—her mom packed up all her stuff and gave it to Goodwill. Said Erika couldn't leave if she had no clothes. Crazy, huh?"

"You're asking me about crazy?" Connor winked and I kissed his baby-smooth cheek.

"Anyway, Erika's aunt drove us to the Goodwill, and all three of us climbed into the big blue bin to pull out her stuff, so yeah, I've done time in a Dumpster."

"Want to do some more? There are quite a few items I'd like to retrieve." Connor put on a pout and batted his lashes. "And you know your girl can't abide climbing in heels."

I laughed. "So wear flats." When he slid off the bed and dumped the half-full garbage bag at my feet, I wove the tangled necklaces between my toes. "What are you doing?"

"I can't very well drive down to the Sally Ann in my undies, now can I? Help me choose something to wear."

For Victoria Day, it was already hot as hell, so I picked out a capped-sleeved A-line dress, black with white polka dots. With that black *Kiss of the Spider Woman* wig in the closet, a smart crimson lipstick, and the pearls twisted around my toes, my girl Charlotte would look like a million bucks while I fished half her life out of the Dumpster.

SEDUCTION DANCE

Dorothy Freed

Something about the woman in the blue merry widow and matching slave collar caught my attention. I liked the way her panties fit over her pubic mound, and the sleek look of her long dancer's legs, in black thigh-high stockings and four-inch heels. She looked to be in her late twenties, several years younger than I, with huge blue eyes and a head of wiry brown curls fanning out to her shoulders. Her small, perky breasts rode high on her chest; her asscheeks were firm and round. She was very pretty—in a strictly female kind of way. I saw her arrive with a couple, but watched her constantly as she moved gracefully around the room without them, and had the sense she was alone.

I was a little surprised by the strength of my interest in her since I'm kinky, but basically straight. Oh, now and then in scenes with other couples the men might encourage some girl-on-girl play—which was enjoyable, but not really my thing. There's even a term for it: incidental bisexuality. Something I did to please Leon, my husband and Master. I've never sought out a sexual experience with another woman on my own—until I saw the woman in blue at the BDSM party in San Francisco that Saturday night.

The party was a quiet one in a private home on Twin Peaks, with maybe eight or nine couples, not much playing. We'd been there about an hour socializing over wine and snack food; the fully clothed Doms were comparing toys and disciplinary techniques, their women collared and in various stages of undress.

I stood beside Leon's chair. His hand was up my skirt caressing my ass and teasing my pussy lips, as I moved to the beat of Madonna music. I was feeling my inner slut that night; sizzling hot in a blood-red camisole, black miniskirt, and the crotchless, fishnet panty hose we'd purchased in Paris, the year before last.

Across the room the pretty woman swayed her hips to the music. Our eyes met and locked. My bold smile announced my attraction. She bent her head in coy response and flashed me a smile back, showing even white teeth, gazing up at me through her lashes. I saw beyond her good looks when she did that, to the vulnerability in her, and saw that her need, like mine, was to be taken, to be forced to give up control. I imagined her bound and helpless on a bed with her arms and legs wide apart, quivering and exposed, pussy swollen with excitement.

She's charming, I thought, enchanted, as the dormant Top-woman in me stirred, yawned, opened her eyes and began to awaken. Looking at her, I understood how Leon felt when he looked at me—and for the first time in my life, I desired another woman.

Leon noticed the girl-on-girl flirtation. "That's a pretty woman, D." He looked up at me, dark eyes questioning. His hand stroked my leg. "Is she someone you know? Or someone you'd like to know?"

"Someone I'd love to play with, Sir," I confessed, blushing, looking down. A shiver of excitement crawled along my skin.

"Really?" he inquired, brows raised in pretended surprise. "Here you had me convinced for years now you'd just as soon leave the girls alone."

I blushed again and looked directly into his eyes as I was required to when I spoke to him. My voice was thick with desire. "May I, Sir?"

Leon grinned and smacked me hard on the ass. "Go for it, baby. Take her. Bring her back here to me."

"Thank you, Sir," I said, and, eyes on the prize, I began my seduction dance.

Madonna again—"Burning Up"—an insistent, aggressive beat that resonated with my excitement level. Moving with abandon, I kept time to the music, grinding my hips suggestively, thigh, ass and belly muscles engaged; shoulders, arms and breasts swaying. My long auburn curls tumbled over my shoulders as I danced. My green predator eyes were fixed on the woman's innocent blue ones. I had her full attention now. She was moving in sync with me.

I couldn't stop smiling as I danced ten feet and eight feet and six feet from her. People picked up on the heat level between us and turned to watch. Tuning them out, I continued, high on excitement, until I'd danced my way across the room and stood before her—so up close and personal, I could feel her body heat.

She was trembling with arousal and cleared her throat nervously, waiting for my next move. I reached out and put my arms around her trim waist, drawing her even closer, tilting my head back to kiss her full on the lips. They were soft and warm and yielded to the thrust of my tongue. I explored her mouth, licking at her teeth and the insides of her cheeks, sucking on her tongue. Her little breasts brushed my full ones, sending electric shocks throughout my body. My breasts were heavy with sensation, my nipples as hard as stones. The woman's furry pubic mound pressed against me. We were thigh to thigh, belly to belly. My breath caught in my throat. My pussy pulsed with excitement.

"I'm D," I said, nuzzling her neck.

Sophia blushed and whispered her name.

"Are you free to join me and my Master?" I asked, indicating Leon. Sophia smiled at his dark good looks, turned back to me and shyly nodded yes.

"And do you want to join me and my Master?" I prodded, making her say it out loud.

"Yes," she said in the smallest of voices, eyes downcast. She blushed again and shifted her weight from one high-heeled foot to the other. She was adorable.

"Yes, *D*," I corrected firmly and made her look at me when she repeated it.

"Come with me," I said, taking her hand. Still bumping and grinding to the beat of the music, I danced Sophia back across the room to Leon, like a lioness returning to the den with her prey.

"What are you going to do with her?" Leon wanted to know after introductions and initial negotiations were made.

I'd thought about that on my way across the room. "May I show you, Sir?"

He nodded, and I led Sophia to a bedroom down the hall; I'd noticed it earlier in the evening when our host showed us around. A four-poster bed dominated the center of the room. There were black sheets on it, and black wrist and ankle cuffs secured to the bedposts. Sophia's eyes widened when she saw it and she drew in her breath. She turned to me, half frightened, but I smiled and kissed her, stroking her hair and pretty, round ass until she relaxed a little.

"Panties off. Now," I ordered. "I want you facedown. Arms and legs spread."

Sophia smiled, and she stared at me through her lashes. "Yes, D," she said, and obeyed.

Leon sat comfortably in the upholstered chair in the corner of the room. He watched with interest as I cuffed Sophia to the bed. She turned her head to me with a *What have I gotten myself into?* look on her face, as her last limb was immobilized and she lay helplessly bound. Looking down at her, I felt a rush of excitement wash over me. I slipped two fingers inside her opening. She was dripping. I could smell her arousal—sweet, musky, intoxicating—like exotic perfume.

She sighed, unresisting, closing her eyes. Her ass looked so inviting I caressed it, tracing along her crack with my fingertips, making her writhe with pleasure. She gasped when I began spanking her, bringing the flat of my hand down hard on her asscheeks. Five sharp slaps spaced wide apart—and five more, fast and hard. She squealed, grinding her clit against the sheets. The slaps stung my hand and I looked toward Leon and his bag of toys.

"Here, D, try these. They're your favorites, aren't they?" He grinned, handing me a wooden paddle, a long-handled leather slapper and a small rubber whip.

I lost track of time as I focused on teasing and tormenting Sophia—delighting in turning her ass and thighs bright red, in hearing her cries and yelps and pleas for mercy—and keeping her right on that magical edge where pain and pleasure merge.

Later, I repositioned her on her back, cuffing her spread-eagled on the bed. She eyed me expectantly, breathing hard, stomach quivering, hips bucking against the black sheets. Kneeling on the bed between her legs, I gazed at the moist, pink opening before me. Her pussy lips were swollen with excitement; her stiff little clit peeked out at me from beneath her pubic hair.

God, she's pretty, she smells so good, I thought. I inhaled deeply, breathing her in—kissing, sucking, stroking, licking her from clit to ass with the flat of my tongue. Reaching up, I seized her nipples, pinching them firmly, rolling the hard little nubs of flesh between my thumbs and forefingers.

Sophia was breathing hard, her head thrown back, hair splayed out on the pillow. "Oh, my god, please don't stop," she moaned, gasping for breath as her orgasm built. I felt her stiffen, her inner muscles clenched. She screamed as she came, arms and legs straining against her restraints. I continued to kiss and stroke and soothe her, until she'd quieted down and her breathing returned to normal.

"That was beautiful, D," Leon whispered in my ear from behind me. He caressed my shoulders and kissed my neck. "You're a good top. I'm impressed. Now, bend over the bed, feet on the floor, ass high. Your girl gets to watch me fuck you."

I obeyed and his cock slid in, filling me, his hands firm on my hips holding me in position. I moaned with pleasure and opened to him. He plunged in to the hilt and my cunt squeezed down on him. His balls spanked my clit as he pumped me. Sophia's eyes met mine. We smiled and held our gaze until Leon grabbed my long red hair and held me by it. I felt my eyes glaze over as my orgasm built, and built, and finally washed over me like a tidal wave.

I'm a screamer, too.

I uncuffed Sophia, kissing her wrists and ankles as I freed them. I had her kneel and service Leon in the armchair while

I watched from the bed, loving the sight of her at his feet, ass up, head bent, sucking him. I could tell he was close to coming when he leaned his head back against the upholstered pillow and closed his eyes. He came in her mouth, with a long, low groan.

We curled up together on the couch in the living room after that, sipping wine, talking, celebrating our meeting and what turned out to be one of the most memorable nights of my life. Later, before long good-night kisses, we made plans to see Sophia again.

"What a surprise," I told Leon, pressing up close to him on the drive home. "I'm not only bisexual, but a switch in the bargain. Did you know that about me all along, Sir? Is that why you encouraged me to go get Sophia?"

"I figured you just hadn't met the right woman before," Leon said. "And when I saw how turned on you were when you saw Sophia, it looked to me like she was the one."

A LITTLE FUN

Rachel Kramer Bussel

Can I buy you a drink?"

He can't be serious, Dee thinks, willing herself not to roll her eyes. Yes, she'd entered a straight bar, wanting a beer or three and some quiet, to watch the game, maybe, to be alone, but in public. Did she look like the kind of woman who wanted a man to buy her a drink? Her fashion sense since she'd turned fifteen had been all about *not* looking that way. She didn't want to be the kind of girl who men thought they owned, simply because she existed. That wasn't why she was gay, but it was at least part of why she was butch, along with the fact that it felt natural, right, the way all the ads in Hannah's magazines and on TV always said a "real woman" should feel. Well, damn it, Dee was a real woman, she just wasn't a girlie one.

Fuck. She was here to think about anything but Hannah, who had lit out of New York the week before, insisting she needed to go to L.A. to pursue her acting dreams. Dee said she would make plans to move out there with her if that's what

Hannah truly needed to be her best self, but Hannah had pressed her delicate, hot pink-painted fingernail against her lips and looked deep into her girlfriend of five years' eyes, and Dee knew. They were over, whether Dee liked it or not. She'd had to hold back her tears, determined not to let Hannah know how much she ached. That was also part of her butchness; she wasn't sure why, exactly, that's just how it was and had always been for her. The femmes cried on her shoulder; if Dee had to cry, it happened in private. That had been six weeks ago, and she was sick of crying.

"Sure. A Guinness. Or whatever," she said, trying not to sound quite so morose. As the guy leaned over the counter, she looked at him. He didn't look gay—of course, as a good queer, she knew you could never really know for sure until you asked, and sometimes not even then, but everyone has tells, even the militantly straight men who secretly wanted to suck cock. There was usually something. This guy just seemed, well, friendly. He had on worn jeans, cowboy boots, a red, orange and white faded flannel shirt over a white T-shirt.

"Here you go," he said, and then he grinned.

"Are you trying to flirt with me?" The words burst out of Dee's mouth before she realized quite how harsh they sounded. They weren't a girl's/woman's words; there was no uptick at the end of the question, no accompanying flirtatious smile or toss of long, glossy hair—Dee didn't have any of the latter, but if she did, it would be worn down her back in one long braid, like she had in junior high, when her mother insisted she keep it well past her shoulders.

"So what if I am?" he asked, raising an eyebrow. He wasn't laughing at her—he was challenging her. Dee's face flushed— she had her tells, as well—and she was annoyed that she was, somewhere, somehow, getting just a little turned on. Had a male stranger who wasn't overtly gay ever flirted with her like this? She'd have to ponder that one later. She was so used to being the one to make the first move, flirting with women, mostly femmes, the occasional androgynous type, a few trans guys who always made Dee feel old. She looked every bit of her forty years, and she didn't mind; her body was strong and she'd packed a lot into her life so far.

"Look, I really appreciate this"—Dee held up the cold, frosty glass—"but I'm gay. Into girls. Women. Queer. In case you couldn't tell." She gestured down at her outfit and willed herself not to blush when she saw that her nipples were hard beneath her white tank top and T-shirt. It was summer, and she hated wearing a bra and tried to avoid it whenever she could.

"That's cool. My sister's a dyke. I just...I don't know, you looked like you could use someone to talk to. And you looked... like my type." At that he blushed, then took a long swig from his glass.

Now Dee was too curious to ignore this man's madness. "I'm your type? What do you mean? Do you have a lot of success with women who look like me?"

"Actually, not so much, but that doesn't mean I've stopped trying. And Janet, my sister, well, sometimes her friends, when they're hard up, when they just want a roll in the hay, we, um, get together. She calls herself my pimp."

"And that's it? Just one-night stands for dykes looking for a little cock?" The word *cock* hung in the air between them.

"It's not so little, I'll have you know. And I'm Brad, by the way." He let his size linger between them; Dee would've been a saint not to wonder whether he was telling the truth.

She took a deep breath. "Okay, fine, I get why they'd be up for it, but what about you? Are you just one of those player types? Wham-bam-thank-you-ma'am? Are you only looking for quickies?" She wasn't hostile or upset, just curious, because Dee was exactly the opposite. She hated that she got so attached, and she could do so before she'd even fucked someone. All a girl had to do was capture her mind and smile at her in a certain way and she was a goner. She'd been a serial monogamist for twenty years; there were two wild years after she left home at eighteen, and then it was strictly serious, intense relationships for her.

"I don't even know why I'm telling you this, but no, actually. I'm not that type of guy at all. I want a real relationship, the kind where we hold hands at the movies and buy birthday presents and meet each other's families and maybe have babies and all that. Sometimes I meet straight girls who seem like they'd be into that, usually sporty types, but I don't know, there's something about all of you"—he tossed his hand out at her. "You're different. You're not trying to please me. I mean, the women I've been with aren't rude or mean or anything, they're just self-contained. They know what they want, which is awesome—except usually it's not me, except in the sack."

Dee listened patiently, sipping her beer, finding herself both sympathetic and, yes, increasingly intrigued in more than a platonic way. She'd never met a straight guy like Brad. Even the gay guys she knew were usually more overtly sexual. He seemed like the stereotype of a sensitive New Age guy, except he was actually interesting. "Don't tell me—you like Sarah McLachlan and all that Lilith Fair crap," she said.

"More like Dylan and Joni Mitchell. I'm a sucker for an acoustic guitar. I play a little myself."

"What do you do for a living?"

"Are you really interested or...?" he asked, leaning forward, that quirky look back on his face.

"Not like that," Dee lied. "But you bought me a drink; I should show a little curiosity, right?" The longer they talked—

through two more rounds that made Dee feel very mellow, like she could melt into the chair—the more she realized she really was interested, and, even better, she wasn't wondering what Hannah was up to, whether she was on the fast track to stardom. She wasn't even sure she wanted Hannah to succeed; it was a mean thought, but she couldn't handle seeing her ex plastered all over ads in the subway, not just yet. Maybe if she were there with her, by her side—Dee didn't care about fame or its trappings, she just wanted to work hard and play hard, and had wanted Hannah next to her while she did at least the latter—but Hannah had made it clear that Dee was too much baggage to bring to the Hollywood Walk of Fame.

Fine, then, Dee thought, when her thoughts inevitably slid toward Hannah, but the drinks were helping ease her to the sidelines, and ease Brad front and center. He was a little dorky—weren't all guys?—but she got the sense that he wasn't trying to con her, that his spiel wasn't some elaborate concoction designed to woo his way into her pants. He wanted her, that much was clear, but he wasn't going to make a fool out of himself, or her, to get her, and that, more than anything, made him different from the average guy she'd observed over the years acting like his dick would fall off if he didn't find a woman to stick it in. At first, she'd been a little bit sympathetic, as Dee knew what it was like to lust after a woman, but she prided herself on not being so foolish as to give up her dignity in her quest for pussy. She wasn't about to give it up for cock, either, but still, she couldn't deny the stirring inside her. How long had it been—twenty years?

She grinned to herself, and Brad caught it. "Laughing at me—or with me?" A smile danced on his lips, and suddenly they weren't laughing at all.

"Come here," she said, and he stepped closer and she grabbed him for a kiss. His lips were a little chilly, but inside, his mouth was warm. At first, she kissed him the way she'd kiss any new conquest, pouncing, taking, demanding. And at first, Brad let her, but soon, he was kissing her back, his fingers sliding through her sleek, short hair. There wasn't enough of it for him to grab on to—his was richer, thicker, longer—but the sensation made Dee moan into his mouth. He was playing her like an instrument, but she liked it. Dee realized she wanted to be played—and played with—because Brad seemed to genuinely be enjoying it, not just trying to get her to give him something so he could take something else. For the most part, that had been her experience of sex with guys.

They kissed until she was breathless and had to lean on him. That did make her feel a bit girlie, but she didn't care. They made it back to his place in a daze, and Dee found herself feeling shy. She would've been annoyed with herself for feeling shy except that it was also kind of hot. "Can we turn off the lights?" she asked, when he started to take off her clothes, after shucking his coat and shirt to reveal a muscular, slightly hairy chest.

"No, we can't, Dee," Brad said, a bit more force and huskiness in his voice. "Then I wouldn't get to see what you've got under there." She'd never have admitted it to him, but she liked the fact that he was being insistent, demanding, not simpering or giggling or any of the other ways girls sometimes were with her.

Brad peeled off her layers until Dee was topless, her heavy breasts hanging there. She settled back against the pillows and soon he was sucking on each nipple in turn, using his entire mouth to make her nipples wet, hard and sensitive. Dee bunched her hands in the pillows as he savored each nub, pausing occasionally to pull back and toy with them with his teeth, watching as his tongue flipped against her hard flesh. He didn't stop even when she tried not so firmly to move his head aside; she didn't really want him to stop, but it seemed polite, since she knew from his bedside clock that it had been at least half an hour. "I'm not done," he gasped roughly, taking her hand and placing it over his jeans so she could feel that he not only didn't mind feasting on her nipples, he liked it.

Dee latched on to his hardness, eager to do something, to contribute in some way, rather than just lie back and take it. It just wasn't in her nature, but finally, when he pressed both of her nipples together and crammed them in his mouth, she sank back and let him make her pussy wetter than she could remember it being in years. Each lick of his tongue was magic, and when he finally let her breasts fall back against her body and moved to kiss her, Dee couldn't believe it. All that talk about girls being better in bed than guys? Well, not when it came to Brad. He slid on top of her and soon had her pants off.

He reached for a condom and stopped to ask her, "Is this okay?"

"Yes, please," she said, and spread her legs wide, even holding herself open for him, something she'd never done in her life. She suddenly wished she didn't have such a big bush, not because she was ashamed, but because she wanted him to see every bit of her, see her totally bare.

"You're so wet, Dee; so, so wet." He looked into her eyes as he spoke, and Dee looked back, smiling as he filled her, his cock as impressive inside her as it had been in her hand. She got fucked and fucked herself plenty, but this was different. Not more "real," just more male—very, very male. Brad was propped up on his elbows, and at first, seemed to be trying to enact some artful dance, making his cock enter her at an angle that she was sure couldn't be comfortable.

"Lean on me. Please. All of you," she said, coaxing him to lie down fully on top of her and give himself to her, all of him, not just his cock. She hugged him with her arms, her legs, her lips pressed against his neck, her nose in his hair, smelling him. She squeezed tightly, shifting against his thrusts, fucking him back just as eagerly as he fucked her. Dee was surprised to find a few tears trickling down her face as she came, trembling, in his arms. That wasn't supposed to happen—or rather, none of this was "supposed" to happen, but it was.

"That's it, yeah, you feel so good," he said, again lifting himself up to truly look at her and swipe some of the tears away. He eased all the way out and she felt the loss in her body, shocked at missing him so, but all Brad was doing was read-justing himself. He lifted her legs onto his shoulders, and pressed himself back down as if she were some size-two model type rather than a beefy butch. Brad ran his hands along her calves, kissed them, then brought his hands down to massage her upper thighs and her ass. His hands felt so good that Dee knew she was going to come again. She wasn't embarrassed, exactly, but she wanted him to come, too; wanted to feel it just as badly as she'd ever wanted to make a girl come and feel the rush of warmth and pride that entails. She squeezed him, closing her eyes to better focus, picturing his cock spurting all over her.

"I want to feel you come on me," she told him. "Not now, another time, I want you to hold your cock in your hand and jerk off on me." Where was this coming from? It wasn't a fantasy she'd ever consciously had in her life, but there it was, what she wanted from Brad, this virtual stranger.

"Oh, yeah? You want me to rub my cock all over you and tease you with it, Dee?" He wasn't laughing at her, as he might have done; in fact, he sounded as breathless as she felt.

"Yes, yes," she groaned as his body shifted again, his hands coming down on her wrists, clamping her in place. She growled and lightly pressed back against him, making his hold on her even firmer. He fucked her more deeply, pounded into her, and when she said, "I want you to come all over my face," he lost it, letting out what felt like a lot of his come into the condom. Dee knew her cheeks were burning, but she didn't care. It was amazing all the images Brad had suddenly planted in her mind.

He collapsed on top of her and she stroked his hair, wet with sweat, his chest hair tickling hers. After a few minutes, he slipped out of her and nuzzled against her, curling his taller body to fit. She wrapped her arm around him and as he drifted off to sleep, snoring lightly, Dee lay there, wide-awake. This was just for fun, right? A way to get Hannah off her mind— Hannah who hadn't been in her head since she and Brad had first kissed hours ago. When Dee started to get up to get her clothes, to go back to her real life, her dyke life, Brad held her tighter. She wasn't sure if he was really sleeping and it was an instinctual move, or if he was awake and pretending to sleep to keep her there.

She looked down at him and let herself smile. Could this be more than a one-night stand? The butch and the dyke-lover, or whatever Brad called himself? She wasn't sure, but she let herself fall asleep. At the very least, she could wait and see what happened in the morning. She was pretty sure Brad's cock would be ready to go. The rest, they could figure out later.

TRINITY

Jordana Winters

I like the tatt."

"What's that?" Carmen turned around to face the stranger.

"Your tattoo," the woman said, referring to the Celtic tattoo Carmen had on her lower back.

"Thanks," Carmen replied, and turned back to her locker.

In the locker room after her workout with her shorts off, Carmen had been standing there in her panties as the woman came around the corner. She'd given Carmen the once-over before stopping at her own locker, which was directly behind Carmen's.

Carmen had seen her before. Her body was a picture of perfection. To say she was toned would be an understatement—she was ripped from head to toe. She always wore short shorts and a sports bra that showcased her ridiculously cut abs.

Carmen watched her walk through the gym with a feline grace. She observed that both men's and women's eyes followed the other woman wherever she went and seemed to scrutinize her every move. She commanded attention with her confidence and self-assurance. She clearly knew she was hot, yet she pulled it off without being cocky, just proud.

If they could tear their eyes off her body they'd realize she was also very pretty. She had a Bettie Page haircut, only shorter, which suited her deliciously. Her skin was pale and appeared flawless. To be sure—she was a looker.

"Do you have any more?" she asked.

"One. Between my shoulder blades."

"Can I see?"

"Sure."

Carmen turned around and pulled up her shirt.

"That's very pretty. I've always wanted one. Only I can't decide where," she said.

"It would suit you."

Carmen turned and stole a glance at the woman through the mirror that hung on the wall across from them. The woman's eyes shot up quickly. She'd been checking out Carmen's ass.

"Not exactly my most flattering pair," Carmen said, referring to her panties—blue and white striped bikinis, one of her least sexy pairs.

"You must be joking. You look great. Your legs are fantastic."

"Thank you," she replied, and turned to look at her as she pulled on her pants.

"Can I buy you a drink sometime?" she asked.

"Yeah, sure. That would be great."

"I'm Trinity."

"Trinity? That's an unusual name."

"I had it legally changed. It was Mary. My parents are crazy religious. I'm the black sheep because they couldn't convert me. Hated my name and everything it represented my entire life," she explained, her eyes intense.

"Isn't Trinity a crazy religious name?"

"Clever girl. It is. It's also from the movie *The Matrix*. I ignore the possible religious connotation."

Carmen dug around in her purse for a scrap of paper and pen, wrote down her number and handed it to Trinity.

"Are you going to tell me your name?"

"It's Mary."

"Tell me you're joking," Trinity said, and rolled her eyes.

"Yeah, I am. It's Carmen."

"Quick witted. I like that," she replied, and smiled broadly. "I'll call you."

"Great. Take it easy."

True to her word, Trinity called the following day. They talked on the phone for a bit before agreeing to meet for coffee. Following their coffee date they met again for dinner.

Carmen couldn't figure out why Trinity wasn't in a relationship. She had everything going for her, a great job and a new condo. She really had her shit together. Aside from that, she was one of the most captivating people Carmen had ever met. She was incredibly intelligent and had something to say about everything from her opinions on the legalization of gay marriage to her thoughts on the downward spiral of "today's society." She thought outside of the box. Carmen was instantly infatuated with her, and the feeling seemed mutual.

They stayed at the restaurant for nearly three hours and left only because the waiter hinted enough times that the restaurant was getting busy and he needed their table.

After the restaurant they had coffee and shared a piece of pie at a nearby café. They'd already shared dessert at the restaurant.

"I feel like a giant pig," Carmen said, and placed her fork on the now empty plate.

"Screw it. Between us it was only one dessert. Besides, it's okay to be gluttonous now and then."

Carmen sat back in her chair and rubbed her belly.

"I suppose you're right."

"Of course I am. So—I'm still in the newlywed stage with my condo. I want to show it off."

"Now?"

"Sure."

Carmen stood close behind Trinity as she unlocked the door. Once she stepped over the threshold she knew their evening was about to take an interesting turn.

Trinity dropped her keys, coat and purse to the floor and pounced on Carmen. In a second, Trinity had her hands locked tightly around Carmen's wrists and had her pinned up against the wall. With their bodies pressed tightly together, and aware of the shape Trinity was in, Carmen knew she wasn't going anywhere.

They were standing nearly nose to nose now, both breathing heavily. Trinity's movements were slow and deliberate as she moved her lips to Carmen's neck, kissing and biting it playfully.

"You smell nice," she purred.

A deep guttural noise emitted from Carmen's throat, a mix of pleasure and pain.

"I know you like me. You do, don't you?" she asked, already knowing the answer.

"Yes."

"Then stop fighting me. Relax," Trinity hissed in her ear.

She'd been standing stiffly and was panting because she'd forgotten to breathe. Carmen exhaled loudly and let her body relax into Trinity's.

"That's better. You've been with women before?" she asked.

"Yes. Sort of."

"Tell me about it," she coaxed and moved so their lips were only inches apart. Her breath smelled of peppermint and faintly of coffee.

"You kissed her?" she asked.

"Yes."

"Show me how."

Trinity's kiss was soft and warm. Ahhhhh...yes. She remembered it now. Only a woman kissed like this—with patience and feeling.

"Tell me more," Trinity demanded.

Her firm grip around Carmen's wrist eased. Her fingertips trailed up the side of Carmen's body, grazing the side of her breast along the way before it came to rest lightly around her throat.

"It was at a house party. She was pretty drunk. I'd had wine—just enough for a good buzz."

Trinity kissed and bit at her neck while she moved her other hand to Carmen's waist and grabbed a handful of her skirt. Her hand moved up under the skirt and traced the tips of Carmen's stockings. Her fingertips over Carmen's bare skin sent heat directly to her sex.

"We were in the dark, alone on a couch in the sunroom. We made out, felt each other up. I'd just gotten my hand into her panties when a guy walked in, whistling and yelling about girl-on-girl action. I didn't need an audience. She felt sick and left to puke."

"Was her pussy shaved?"

Her hand moved down over Carmen's breast and under her shirt. Her other hand moved farther up between her thighs.

"Not totally."

"Is yours?" she purred, and kissed her again.

Her hand cupped Carmen's sex, moved up to the top of her panties and slipped inside.

"Lovely..."

Carmen had shaved a few days ago, leaving very little stubble.

"You're very wet."

Trinity's finger grazed over her clit lightly. Truly, this was how it should be done—light and teasing as opposed to clumsy and impatient.

"And you?" Carmen asked and reached for Trinity's belt. She undid it quickly, along with her pants.

She teased just as Trinity had, first sliding her hand down the outside of her panties, then rubbing her gently. Her panties were, in fact, quite wet.

"And shaved?" she asked, as she moved her hand into Trinity's panties and found her cunt to be as trimmed as her own.

Carmen moved her fingers over Trinity's clit while Trinity's fingers continued their assault on her cunt. They were finger-fucking in perfect synchronization, moving and thrusting their hips while pulling off each other's clothes.

Carmen's shirt was open, her bra around her neck with her skirt and panties crumbled around her feet. Trinity had kicked her panties and pants off and had, with Carmen's help, pulled her shirt off.

No longer shy, their kisses were wild and passionate, their bites harder and likely to leave bruises tomorrow.

Carmen turned Trinity around so their positions were reversed, with Trinity now pressed against the wall. She grabbed hold of a nearby chair and pulled it close, spilling envelopes and mail on the floor in the process.

"Put your leg up," Carmen growled.

Down on her knees on the hard floor, Carmen had a face full of pussy. Trinity's lips were soft and puffy, full and engorged. Her scent was musky and delicious. Again, she kissed and sucked, fingered and fucked, while Trinity coaxed her, mewling and telling her, "Yes," and "Fuck, right there."

Trinity came on quivering legs, yelping and panting, holding on to Carmen to keep her up.

Trinity grabbed hold of Carmen, pushed her down on the chair, spread her legs and ate her pussy. Shit. This was how it should be done. Trinity nipped, teased and licked all the right spots. This needed to be taught to men everywhere. This was the real fuckin' deal.

With her hands holding on to the chair until it hurt, Carmen came, not once but twice, her legs a quivering mass banging against Trinity's ears.

"Fuck!" Carmen said loudly.

Trinity laid her head on Carmen's belly. Carmen wrapped her legs tightly around her while smoothing her hair.

"That was really good," Trinity muttered into her belly button.

"Mmmm," she moaned in agreement.

"Come on. Let's lie down."

She took Trinity's hand and followed her to her bedroom. They snuggled up together under her deliciously soft comforter.

"Stay the night with me."

She had wondered if Trinity would offer and she'd already decided she wouldn't decline. She was falling hard for this woman.

"You sure?" she asked.

"Yeah. I have an extra toothbrush. You can borrow anything.

Just one of many reasons why fucking a woman is better—I'll always have toilet paper and if you want to borrow my deodorant you won't smell like Old Spice."

Carmen giggled, kissed her and snuggled closer.

"You're really fuckin' cool, Trinity."

"Thank you."

And then, they slept.

MEETING AT THE HOLE IN THE WALL

Aimee Pearl

The First Time

I have my period, but he is so eager to eat me that he pulls out my tampon with his bare slippery fingers and dives in; no one has ever done that before.

I let him because I figure, safety-wise, he is the one taking the risk. It is my blood, not his. I know I don't have anything. As for what he knows, I guess he just doesn't give a shit. I also let him because he knows what he is doing, and he is good at it.

But first let me tell you how we got to this point. I met him online while looking for something kinky, and his pervertedness did me in. It's rare that a man can make my clit hard with merely a few well-turned phrases about spanking. He had my attention.

He invited me over for dinner. Well, he asked me first if I was hungry; unceremoniously, he stated that he was going to order takeout before fucking me. I declined the food, not just as a girlie-coyness thing, but because it was late and I had already eaten.

When I arrived, it turned out he had taken me at my word. He had a whole bunch of food for himself, and nothing for me. Somehow, this turned me on even more. Chivalry is dead, and I want to writhe naked on its grave.

He ate his dinner while I ate nothing. The rudeness I crave doesn't have to take place only in bed—it can last all day. It's foreplay, candy. I'll still want to crawl across the floor for the chance to lap from your puddle of piss.

He was a husky thing, with a big appetite. We sat on his couch, to-go boxes propped on his coffee table. There was not much pausing for breath between his bites, and definitely no conversation. No TV, either. I was just to sit there, waiting. He practically ignored me as he stuffed his face, and I squirmed ever so slightly, getting wetter by the second beside him, waiting until it was my turn to get his attention, waiting until he discovered I was not wearing any panties.

He finished his meal. Shoved the boxes away. Leaned back against the cushions. And announced, "After a meal like that, I like to get my cock sucked." He put his hand on his lap and began stroking the rigid mass under his jeans. My eyes bulged, and before I could even say anything, he had a fistful of my hair and was shoving my mouth down onto his crotch. "Get the fabric wet," he ordered. "Show me how badly you want to put it in your mouth."

I dutifully complied.

The Next Time, a Year Later

He's got his hands around my throat, and I study his expression. His eyes are half-closed in concentration, and the look on his face is a mixture of determination and bliss. He might be as hard as I am wet. He bears down, fingers pressing in. My hands clutch at his. Four hands at my neck. I feel like I'm going to pass out.

He mixes his brutality with grace. He's only doing this because I asked him to. I asked him, "Can I put your hand on my throat?" Then I took his hand and put it there. He followed with the other.

He keeps saying he won't fuck me tonight. His roommate is on his way home, they have plans, and I have to go. But sometimes a good choke is better than a good fuck. And either way I end up wet.

He's strong, and he could kill me.

I had come to his house earlier in the evening. He texted me, ordering me to come to him. It was very last-minute, and I felt conflicted about dropping everything to follow his orders. But the physicality of what we do together compels me.

When I arrived, I did some housework for him, then gave him a massage. I like to be bossed around, to be told what to do and then do it. Now he's choking me and next he's going to drive me to the train station.

When he first saw me tonight, he told me I looked cute. And later, he mentioned I had a nice ass. (But that's a given. Everybody likes my ass. Even the gayest gay men would go bi for my ass—and have.) But even with these compliments, I have this idea that he's not attracted to me, because he calls for me so rarely. So I feel like I'm compromising myself to be with him. I mean, why be with someone if he's not that into me, and if he *is* into me, why does he call me so infrequently? And I can't call him, because that's not the game. The game is: he's in charge, and I follow instructions. The trouble is, I'm always ready to play, but the ball is always in his court.

I like rough sex with a certain flavor that's hard to come by. A friend of mine who's also a masochist is always talking about how hard it is to find a good sadist. How rare they are. How masochists vastly outnumber sadists, and how sadists can have their pick of whomever they want and we masochists just have to be happy with what we get. I think I've started to believe her...

I tend to see myself, for better or worse, through the eyes of my lovers. One guy I'm with makes me feel like the most beautiful woman on the planet. Another woman, a friend of mine "with benefits," makes me feel smart and fun to be around. But this guy makes me feel like I'm lucky to even get his time. It's wreaking havoc with my self-esteem. What's wrong with me? Have I internalized the sadist/masochist dynamic to the point where I actually put him above me *in real life*? And why do I crave even the slightest attention from this man?

Part of me wants to walk away, but the other part just wants to kneel at his feet. He's sexy, and he's unbearably good in bed. So good he should give classes in what he does. Except it seems so innate, I don't think it can be taught. His sexuality operates on a whole different level from anyone I've been with, and I feel intense chemistry with him.

It's getting late, and I'm at his house, and he's choking me and pushing me away.

The Third Time
   "I'm going to start by shoving my cock in your ass."
   He has one hand gripping my chin.
   "I'm going to fuck you roughly, and it's going to hurt."
   His other hand is covering my mouth.
   "You're not allowed to scream. I have neighbors."
   He increases the pressure from his hands.
   "Do you understand?"
   I nod slowly. He smiles and nods with me, and then uses his hands to move my head up and down, as though I am actually nodding faster and more vigorously.

"That's right. You do understand. You understand that I'm going to use you, and you're going to take it. Ready?"

The Last Time

We meet up at a gay leather bar in the SoMa district. It's my idea, and it seems appropriate. We haven't seen each other in six years, almost to the day, by his calculation. He remembers everything. He recalls it to me. That puts me at ease, because then I don't feel embarrassed for having memorized it, too.

Our history was so brief. Only a few encounters. But each of them so memorable, they are etched on our brains together. He reminisces aloud, and in my head, sliding into an increasingly comfortable space, so do I.

There is only one other woman in the bar, and she doesn't stay there for long. So the gay leather daddies keep looking at us. We are obviously together, and even seemingly heterosexual because we are a man and a woman. Little do those guys know: we're probably queerer and kinkier than all of them put together.

Put together. I want to put us together. I want him to drag me by the neck into the cum-and-piss-stained bathroom and fuck me against a grimy stall wall.

There is some flirting, light touching and then kissing. I guess the reminiscing had the same effect on both of us. He hadn't been planning to take me home with him, but he seems to have changed his mind about that pretty quickly. I hadn't planned on going home with him. I had planned on closure, and on showing off the self-esteem I've built up over these years, and on leaving the bar proud that I don't need his mean hands. But I changed my mind about that pretty quickly, too. The chemistry is just too intense to ignore.

In the bar, kissing on the bench by the pool table, he's shoving his tongue in my mouth, and it's thick and luscious. "This is how men kiss," he says. "Men are gross. Men are pigs. They do this." And his tongue slides in again. "I like it," I say.

He's hard and eager to get me home now. Drives fast. Touches my thigh. I want him inside me. I feel tongue-tied.

At his house, there's suddenly a lot of messing around with his cats. Feeding them. Putting them out in the backyard. Finally, he's ready. He takes me into the bedroom and orders me to take off his boots. I think about how much I would like to feel his boot on my clavicle. He gives me directions on how to keep them tidy ("Pull the laces back up and put them inside...") and where to put them after I take them off ("on a low shelf by the door, as bookends to the books on that shelf"). Then he takes off his pants and explains how he likes them to be hung ("hook, button, and zip up"). I hang them.

I'm standing by the bed, and he bends me over, plays with my pussy through my jeans, rubs against me. He orders my jeans off. Spits on my ass, just to show ownership. He moves around to face me but then grabs me by the back of the head and shoves my face against his boxer briefs. I can feel his hard cock on the other side. Lifting me up, he pinches my nipples, bites and sucks on them, then puts his cock between my tits and rubs it back and forth.

All this is foreplay. Now he gets behind me again, kicks my legs apart and begins to fuck me. Cold lube, warm cunt, and soon he's in deep. I had told him earlier, in the bar, "I have my period. But, it's at the end."

"What?"

"I have my period. But—"

"What?"

"I have my—"

He started laughing, and I realized he already heard me. He

just likes hearing it. He likes it. I remember.

He pulls his cock out to show me how bloody it is. "I thought you said you were near the end," he says. I twist around to look. "I thought I was," I reply meekly.

But he's enjoying it. He smears blood on my asscheeks and down my thighs. He keeps fucking me and then stopping to spread more blood around, and then fucking me again. He calls it a "bloody mess" and says it's "fucking hot, all messy and bloody like that." The only light in the room comes from a candle he lit earlier, and he admires my blood-covered ass and cunt, exposed by my bent-over position, in the flickering glow. Red blood painted on the canvas of my brown skin thanks to this white Diego Rivera. He's a fucking artist, and I have never felt so sexy on the rag before.

He fucks me till he's tired, and I've come a few times, and the cats are meowing loudly and he has to go let them back in.

I clean up and get dressed, and he takes me to the train station. We kiss good-bye in the car, and, suddenly overeager and overanxious, I ask him about next time. He looks away and says he'll email me. I'm sure neither of us believes him. He always leaves me in a state of doubt. Or do I do that to myself?

He is more cruel than kind, and everything he does to me undoes me.

THE STATE

Tahira Iqbal

The funeral cars are nose to tail, stretching down the cemetery path as far as the eye can see. I step out of one, Antonio coming round to meet me with an umbrella, giving me a moment under the steady patter of rain.

My husband slides his hand into mine.

"Ready?"

I kiss him lightly on the lips, nodding as the uncharacteristic shaking in my bones that had made getting dressed in all black this morning a challenge, burrows deeper.

"This day is going to difficult," Antonio says softly, "but we're going to get through it." His ice-blue eyes echo my pain as a cavernous ache tears through me.

I walk the path, following the mourners; my sister is up front. Anna's hand is tight in her husband's grasp, the other holding on to a usually rambunctious five-year-old, who turns around and gives me a big smile. I send one back to my niece—or at least I hope it looks like a smile.

We stand, six deep, listening to the service. My eyes are trained on the casket, how utterly shiny it looks, the rivulets of water rushing down its curves. There's a huge spray of white lilies that go head to foot on top of it, the dedication from my bereft mother.

A desperate catch in my throat makes me close my eyes. "Good-bye, father," I whisper. "Good-bye."

After, we all head to the country estate of one of father's friends, a gesture of comfort at this difficult time. Antonio and I are cleared to enter the building, security is tight; we hadn't buried just any man, we'd buried a man with connections that went high. Seriously high.

I leave my damp coat with a waiting member of the staff and then ask for directions to the bathroom.

I slide the lock into place and lean against the vanity, staring at my shaking hands, taking long breaths, hoping that they go deeper than the middle of my chest. My muscles are tight, locked, loaded with fatigue.

It had been Antonio to lift my cell to his ear; my hands had been covered in flour as we'd prepared dinner.

"Ciao, Anna!" he'd answered cheerily, *"Come stai?"*

I'd carried on preparing the meal, only looking up when I realized that Antonio hadn't spoken for a long while. My blood had run cold because of the look in his glittering eyes.

With a thudding heart, I splash cold water on my face and head back out.

Semi-composed, I find Anna and Rick. "Hey, where's Lily?"

Her parents nod over to the back of the room. I see my niece sitting on my mother's knee, cuddled in tight against her. The tension in my chest sinks even deeper. Mother's eyes had dimmed the moment she'd heard of father's death...and I fear that they may never light again.

"Do you want something to eat?" Anna says.

I shake my head.

"Serafina, please..."

"I'm okay."

"I'm worried about you; Antonio, too."

I follow Anna's line of sight again, finding him in Armani black, drink in hand, talking to some of our relatives.

"Excuse me." I hustle myself out of the room, heart racing again.

I take the opportunity for some air now that the cloud cover has finally broken. The wide rays of sun illuminate the lush gardens wonderfully, so I step down into the greenery, heels spiking the grass as I aim for the aromatic raised beds.

Sensing the presence of another, I turn to see a woman who's wearing mirrored aviators and a fitted black suit with a white shirt. If she didn't have a curly clear plastic wire snaking up her neck and into her ear, I would think she's another mourner.

"You're with the security team? I'm fine."

"With all due respect, my team and I need to ensure your safety, ma'am."

"Ma'am is my mother." I take a step forward, extend my hand. "Call me Sera."

"Cassie."

"Wait, you think that there's a threat against me? Because my father was murdered?"

She nods. "Your father made arrangements for you all; everyone has a dedicated security team of his own. I'm with you and your husband."

"So, you're twenty-four/seven?"

"I am." The striking woman has black hair, pulled into a ponytail that reaches past her shoulders, which are slender just like the rest of her. There are lines around her eyes; I have to wonder if they are from laughter or stress, but I'm guessing it's the latter. I turned thirty-two this year; she doesn't look like far off that.

"I can give you a moment."

I nod my thanks and retreat back into the garden, but she only gives me yards of distance.

It's late afternoon; Anna has opened her home to immediate family and everyone is heading back there.

"I wish you were coming with us." She hugs me with the power of a bodybuilder.

"I want to go home." My eyes clog with tears. "I want to try and start to make sense of this."

"They will find who did this."

I'm suddenly back in the kitchen, flour on my hands, holding my breath, watching Antonio as he disconnects the call.

"Darling..." he'd said, reaching for me, but I'd stepped away, not wanting to hear the words that would match the utter devastation in his eyes.

"Hey, are you all right?" Anna rubs my arm, bringing me back to reality.

"I'm okay."

"I have a bodyguard." She nods to the doorway where a stocky middle-aged man stands with Rick and Lily.

"I know, so do we." I gesture over her shoulder.

"Wow, she looks like she should be on a runway."

I smile. Yeah, I'd thought the same thing.

Antonio and I are driven into the city by Cassie. The blacked-out Escalade slides through the streets with ease, ending up outside our townhouse.

Cassie holds out an envelope that Antonio takes.

"We changed your locks, installed a new security system."

"What? When?" he says.

"Today. It was part of the contract your father-in-law drew up with the company before his death."

"That means he knew something was going to happen…" I murmur to myself.

Antonio rips open the envelope. "*Dios mio,* you guys are really serious…"

"You have my number, but I'll be close."

"How close?" I ask.

"In the home."

"As long as Serafina is safe, I don't care if we have to live in Fort Knox," Antonio says, kissing my temple.

Cassie escorts us to the front door, where Antonio turns the unfamiliar key, retrieves the new alarm code from the envelope and punches it into the panel.

"I'll be in your guest bedroom," Cassie says. "Second floor, right?"

"You've been here?" I say.

"I oversaw the installation."

Prickles of unease trickle through me, hardening the atmosphere.

"Lucky for you we remodeled just last month," Antonio says, aiming to lighten the mood, but all I can see are images from today flashing through my mind. Father's casket. The casket being lowered into the ground. Palming wet earth, tossing it into the grave.

"Hey—are you all right?"

I don't even realize that I'm swaying until Cassie reaches for my elbow to stop me from falling.

"You need to rest," Antonio insists.

"You're safe within these walls, but I'm going to do another walk-through. You're all right?"

I nod and then head upstairs with Antonio, looking back

to see Cassie shrug out of her jacket, a huge gun strapped to her hip.

At three in the morning, Antonio finds me curled on the armchair, staring into space, when I should be beside him.

"Sleep, *amore*," he murmurs drowsily.

"I can't." I rise, kiss his brow, reach for my wrap and head downstairs.

I try to fix myself a snack, but end up banging around the space, slamming drawers, shoving the half-made sandwich in the bin, then leaning against the granite counter. I see a rapid movement out of the corner of my eye. "Shit!"

There's Cassie, wearing only her panties and shirt, a gun pointed in my direction. Her eyes, quick and sharp, assess the room. The occupant. The gun lowers instantly to her side.

I'm not sure if I should be terrified or...thrilled. I've never seen such a beautiful, womanly body. Her powerful leg muscles show me such incredible vitality that I vow to hit the gym harder. Her black panties ride low on her hips, illustrating the soft trace of her abs, but it's her eyes, masked earlier by the aviators, now revealed to me. Dark, like midnight, and trained on me.

"You can put your hands down," Cassie says.

Heat rises to my cheeks as I comply jerkily.

"I heard the noise." Cassie clicks the safety on.

"I didn't think..."

Cassie raises one hand as if to say, No *harm, no foul.*

"I'm really sorry."

"Hey, if it means you're so used to my presence already that you felt it was okay to wreck your kitchen, then it's fine with me." She smiles, looking suddenly incredibly more beautiful, especially with her hair flowing around her shoulders.

I take a slow, sure breath. "Good night, Cassie." I walk past her, the soft strains of her lavender-scented perfume following.

Early the next morning, Antonio and I share breakfast in the kitchen; Cassie's on a call in the den.

"She pulled a gun on you?"

"She thought I was…you know, someone else," I say, refilling our coffees.

"I thought bodyguards who were willing to take a bullet were men."

"Hey, I don't want anyone to take a bullet." My heart swells as I'm reminded of her poised and dangerous figure, her barely there garments and the deadly duty she'd elected to take on our behalf.

Cassie returns, eyes hard. "You better get dressed, both of you." She looks to me. "It's your sister."

Five minutes later, Antonio and I are changed and out of the door with Cassie and into the SUV.

I race through the ER, not bothering to check in at the desk, as I see Rick holding Lily, who's still in her Disney Princess pajamas.

"Is Anna okay?" The man is ghostly, eyes stained with tears.

"Someone came to the house," he whispers. "They shot her."

Antonio has to hold me upright. "Shot Anna?"

"They killed the bodyguard."

"Lily…" I look at the resting child.

"She's okay." Rick kisses the top of her head with relief. "She slept right through it."

I pull away from Antonio. "Where's Anna?" I search for someone to speak to.

"Sera, they took her up to surgery, it's pretty bad."

My legs start to shake; a hand goes to my shoulder. Cassie. "Sit."

And I do.

Four hours later, Lily's awake and in my arms but quiet as

a mouse; Antonio is beside me. Cassie stands with a colleague, someone who'd had enough authority to move us from the public waiting area to a private room on the same floor as Anna's surgery.

The operation has been a success, the bullet removed, but she'd lost her spleen. Rick is with her at the moment.

Cassie flips her phone open; it was her millionth call since we'd arrived at the hospital.

"We've arranged for a safe house for your family."

"What about Anna?"

"We're going to move her to a private medical facility within the hour."

"Okay, I'm going to go with her."

Cassie shakes her head. "We need to keep you apart. Our location is secure—very secure—but we're not taking chances in grouping you together."

"This is my sister! She was shot!" My loud concern makes Lily cry. "We need to stick together."

"We can't risk it."

I battle to keep my composure when Antonio says, "I will go with Anna."

"I'm not leaving you."

He puts his palm against my face. "*Amore,* you need to be safe. You're the CEO at your father's company. Anna's the CFO. Something is going on and we need to understand it."

"You think I'm next?"

"I'm not taking any risks. If Cassie thinks we're better off being apart, then that's what we're going to do."

An hour later, I watch the car collect my family to take them to what I pray is safety. Mother is being moved to another location this very hour, too.

Moments later, I'm with Cassie in her SUV. As we drive in

the opposite direction to my townhouse, I ask her where we're going.

"Out of state. I've had word that your home was broken into."

I find it a challenge to see the road ahead as tears trek down my face, my heart bursting with worry for Anna, for Antonio, for my family. I'd spoken at great length with her surgeon, who was confident that she would be fine despite the travel so soon after surgery.

I'd then kissed Lily, embraced Rick, both of us doing our best to remain calm for his upset daughter. It was with Antonio that I'd sobbed, "I love you."

He'd said, "I love you!" He'd kissed me hard, lovingly and settled me in the care of Cassie. "You keep her safe, promise me."

I'd watched her eyes, the color deepening and utter focus seeping into her tight nod.

"We're here." I blink awake from the shake to my shoulders to see a two-story house set on its own parcel of land.

Morning rain drifts on the horizon as I step out of the car. A clean fresh scent envelopes me.

"Are we near the ocean?"

"We are." Cassie opens the front door, allowing me to pass through first.

The open-plan house is surprisingly stunning—neutral decor on the walls, plush furniture sitting on thick rugs which in turn rest on darkly stained boards.

"This is some safe house." I look around the open-plan living room, an endless horizon visible through the back windows.

"Actually, this is my place; I think our safe houses have been compromised."

I face her quickly. "Your family, we've ensured that they are somewhere safe, I can assure you of that."

"You're sure?" I whisper shakily.

"Look, why don't you go upstairs? Take any room except the first on your right; get some rest."

"I'll just call Antonio." I search through my bag but come up empty.

"I took your cell while you were sleeping. I'm sorry, I can't risk this place being exposed through a trace."

"But..."

"I will get updates." She holds up her phone. "This is a clean cell, and the people looking after your family have this number."

With nothing more to say, I aim for the stairs, muted by the events.

In the guest room, I stand at the window, staring out at a crashing ocean that rolls onto a beach set beyond the sloping garden. Dark clouds pepper the epic horizon, chasing away the sunlight.

I investigate the room absently; there's a comfortable-looking queen-sized bed, an empty walk-in closet, and an en suite. I see the large, glass cubicle, the rainfall showerhead, the body jets. I immediately reach for the hem of my T-shirt and lift it over my head.

Twenty minutes later, feeling a heck of a lot better, and changed back into my clothes, I find myself at the barely ajar door of Cassie's room, hoping to get an update.

The shower switches off and I hear the boards creak in the room. She exits, wrapped in a white towel that barely reaches midthigh. She reaches for another towel, rubbing it over her hair a few times before dropping them both to the floor.

Growing hot, I watch her, long, lean and lovely, as she draws on her basic-black underwear.

Seeing the raw strength in her body, the physique that has been charged to take care of me, makes an intense blush move over my cheeks. I step back, until I reach my room, strange vibrations in my pelvis accompanying me as I lie down.

Sleep brings dreams, distorted images where I'm at Father's side the moment of his murder. His cold hands have tangled with mine and his death rattle is as loud as a siren. I'm then comforted by Antonio in a large, barren hospital where I can see Anna in the distance wired to so many machines that aim to save her life but her blood is still pooling on the floor. Cassie stands beside her in nothing more than her bra and panties, a gun at her side, wearing her earpiece like a necklace.

"It's okay." A voice drifts through my senses.

"Antonio," I cry softly. "Antonio…" I reach for the hand on my shoulder. "I'm scared…" I wake in darkness, reaching forward, pushing my lips against soft, soft skin of a face hidden by the shadows.

Lavender seeps into my senses.

"Oh, god…" My lips are barely inches from hers.

"It's okay. You were having a nightmare?" She switches the bedside lamp on.

I nod, shaking the tears free.

"I'm…" I blush.

Cassie laughs gently, "It's okay."

"I thought you were Antonio."

She smiles warmly as I try to settle my charging heart, but it doesn't work. Her hair is damp; small dark pools of water pepper her navy-blue T-shirt.

I close my eyes. "I want this to be over, to know who did this, to not feel this scared."

Her arms go around my frame and I sink into the embrace, propelled by the furious feelings in my pelvis that feel so different from being intimate with Antonio but utterly familiar as I recall a female lover from my past who'd been my first everything.

She pushes my hair back from my shoulders in a comforting gesture; I reach for her hand, bringing it to my lips, pressing a kiss there. "Thank you for looking after me, my family..."

Her dazzling eyes sparkle. "Why don't you lie back?" she says gently.

I think she's going to leave me alone, but instead she leans down, kissing my brow, working her way down until she finds my lips.

I open my mouth with a groan, welcoming her in, her hands effortlessly working the zipper on my jeans.

With a fractured moan, I shiver, finding that the skill of her hand delving into my panties pushes me to the edge of orgasm with such swiftness that I have to squeeze my eyes shut.

Flickers of heat gain purchase across my skin, all pointed like arrows to the heart of my femininity and in the next second I explode into an orgasm.

Cassie reaches for my shirt, pushing it upward, cupping the lower swell of my breast, her hand snaking behind to unhook my bra, and as I sit up, I drag everything overhead and toss it to the floor.

Her hungry gaze travels down my shape, to the undone fastenings of my jeans.

Her keen hands drag them off and then kisses go from knee to lips in a sexy ascent that has me gasping as her hand does wondrous things between my legs. I'm nearly naked, and the fine cotton of her garments is soft against my skin, but an utter torment.

I kiss her ravenously, unaware of time, unaware of my surroundings. The loud, worrying ache that's been in my head is far in the distance as I dig my toes into the covers, muscles straining to the point of cramping as another orgasm fires through me.

Drained, I hug Cassie to my breast, inhaling the scent of her clean hair as my senses back down and I fall into sleep.

It's dark outside when Cassie's cell vibrates noisily on the nightstand, waking us at the same time.

"They've arrested three men in connection with your father's murder." She scrolls through the text. "There's evidence linking them to Anna."

I sit upright, hugging the blanket she'd drawn over me earlier.

Another text arrives. "You can go home," she says gently. I watch those eyes, bright and wonderful. "It's over."

A new panic slides into my senses as I reach for her, kissing her deeply and fitting myself against her form, pulling at her clothes. Distantly, I'm aware that somewhere in the house, my cell is ringing a tune that I had programmed into it to indicate that Antonio, and only Antonio, is calling. I ache to answer it, as well as Cassie's searching hands that are sliding up my torso and cupping my breast.

STRANGE
STATUS QUO

Salome Wilde

W hen had Selby realized that in Kate she had a voyeur on her hands? More importantly, when had she made up her mind to do something about it?

Not in the early days, certainly, when Kate's attention was so fully on her and her alone. It perhaps couldn't have been otherwise when she was not just playing hard to get, she *was* hard to get—physically and emotionally. Kate was patient and focused, the perfect personal assistant. Selby, by comparison, was impatient and hyperfocused, the perfect historical novelist. She thought only and obsessively of her work, often writing one book while planning the next. Kate, meanwhile, quietly moved into the spare bedroom and kept happily busy, proofreading contracts, exploring new publishing opportunities, planning book-signing tours, even offering editorial advice when invited. And, to Selby's delight, it turned out she could make a superb ham and scallion omelet.

With noses so fully in their own realms of paperwork and

Selby having decided not to decide whether she even had a
sexual orientation, it was astonishing they'd ever gotten into
bed. But Kate's energy was so unwaveringly serene and quietly
seductive that Selby found herself accepting sexual favors
without ever intending to. An evening's book would drop from
her fingertips as Kate quietly padded into the room, her smooth
olive complexion lit only by a reading lamp. She'd slip beneath
the covers to make her way between Selby's plump, pale thighs
before Selby could manage an objection.

Now, three years later, both professional rapport and sexual
pleasures were equally excellent. Selby grew in confidence that
she was, indeed, in possession of a healthy libido, and Kate thor-
oughly enjoyed her position in the household. The two women
had, as the saying goes, an understanding. It did not include
reference to exclusivity. It did not include romance. Yet neither
woman could imagine doing without the other.

Therefore, one late night at a publishers' convention when
Selby had decided to embark on a rare tryst with an attractive
and fawning young man whom she'd brought back to her hotel
room, she was shocked to spy Kate watching them through a
crack in the closet door. Selby said nothing, for Kate had not
seemed to know she'd been spotted and, somehow, rather than
breaking her stride, being watched had made the experience
far more pleasurable. Two fans, Selby concluded: the energetic
man in her bed and the silent woman in the closet. Selby came
and came and came. When she finally escorted the man from
her room and locked the door behind her, she listened for Kate.
Surely she would have to come out and confess her crime. But
she did not, and Selby did not confront her. When she woke
in the morning and opened the closet door, it contained only
her clothes.

Back home, neither spoke of the experience. Life did not

change, either in or out of the bedroom. They worked well together; they made love when Selby wished, and they even slept together now and then. But Selby was eager for the next business trip when she could seek confirmation. She became suddenly interested in the kinds of publishers' events she never had been before. She wondered obsessively: maybe she'd been mistaken; maybe Kate hadn't even been in the closet. She had to know.

Only a few weeks later, they were in a luxury hotel in downtown Chicago. As always, their sleeping arrangements included a suite with two bedrooms joined by a shared front room. Selby checked to be sure the closet door was closed, then spent the day smiling until her face ached at boring sales pitches and suggestions for the next volume in her Civil War epic. When at last the evening came, she was ready to put the test to work. Cruising the establishment's bar brought quick results, for at these conventions Selby was a minor celebrity and could use it to her advantage. No sooner had she shown interest in an editor who was, of course, an aspiring novelist, than Kate suddenly rose to go back to the room. "To make some overseas calls," she clarified. Selby nodded her false belief in the excuse, but the lie made her tingle. Could there be any doubt Kate was headed up to the closet?

Jake Rogashefsky was the founder and head editor of a new and reasonably successful e-press, specializing in the woman-warrior genre. And, of course, he had his own heroine about whom he hoped soon to unveil a trilogy...though he hadn't begun writing it yet. Still, there was something sincerely sweet about the way he praised several of her novels with the kind of detailed reference that made it clear he'd actually read them. It didn't hurt that he had eyes the color of rich chocolate, long black lashes and a head of thick, wavy brown-black hair. Top that off with juicy lips and a body that obviously enjoyed frequent trips to the gym, and Selby was nearly sold. Closing the deal, of course, was simply a matter of reminding herself of who was waiting for her, hidden away and ready to watch.

If Selby wasn't the smoothest seductress, neither was Jake quick to take a hint. But, heart hammering, she finally reached the point when she had enough wine in her to say the necessary words: "Would you like to come up to my room?" Unless the low lighting deceived her, they both reddened at that. But the arrow had hit its mark, and into the elevator they went, Jake taking her hand like a schoolboy and endearing himself further. Nevertheless, it was the thought of Kate that made her squeeze back and kiss him, deep and long, on the ride up to the eighteenth floor.

"Oh, I'm sure she's gone to bed," Selby answered when Jake wondered about her assistant. She'd introduced Kate in the bar, and explained that they shared a suite but—of course—had their own rooms.

"I'll be as quiet as I can," Jake volunteered, turning and pressing Selby against the door as she closed it behind her. One lamp was on and Kate's door was closed. She was quickly distracted, for, as it had been in the elevator, Jake's kiss was passionate and flavored with the scotch he'd been drinking. And now that they were alone he was even more ardent, more self-assured. Selby closed her eyes and enjoyed the anticipation of all that was to come.

Sooner than she thought, she wanted more. Jake had reached inside and up the back of her blouse, then withdrew his hands to unbutton it and stroke gentle fingers over her belly and under her bra. Her nipples grew hard, sending shivers through her. She pulled Jake in close to squeeze his lovely tight buns, and felt the hardness waiting for her in those dress slacks. She took his hand and led him into her room, aiming for the bed in the darkness while her eyes were on the closet. When she saw the door was no longer fully closed, she thrilled, and felt her panties moisten. Amazing how just the tiniest crack, barely visible in the light trickling in from the front room, could make so much difference.

And that difference drove her through one incredible fuck. Once a shy, nearly asexual being, with her delicious little voyeur watching, she was a wild hedonist. She knelt before Jake as he faced the closet and used her teeth to undo his belt and his fly. She watched his pants drop and heard his little gasp of pleasure as she nuzzled into his boxers and sucked his swollen head. Her hands remained on the floor before her, and she raised her ass so she was on all fours, a sensuous animal for Jake, giving Kate what she hoped was a welcome view. Jake threaded his fingers in her hair as she swallowed him down. Looking up, she delighted at the sight of his eyes meeting hers as he emitted a long, low moan. But when it seemed he would come with unexpected quickness, she pulled off and pulled him onto the bed.

Figuring how best to keep their fuck positioned in front of that closet door was a challenge, but Selby rose to it with gusto. She pulled up her skirt and pulled her panties down and off, flinging them at the crack in the door—casually enough, she hoped, not to seem to be intentionally aiming. She almost hoped to hear Kate react, but this was about letting Kate enjoy her voyeurism while she enjoyed her exhibitionism. And Jake. With his sweet face shoved between her widespread thighs, he proved surprisingly talented. She moaned in genuine arousal, and added a bit of dirty talk that made her blush until she came all the harder for it. "Fuck yesss," she hissed, peaking into soft lips and nimble tongue, rocking and riding it out and wishing she could call out Kate's name instead of Jake's.

When he finally climbed on top of her, though, equipped with the condom she gladly supplied, she was ready to be Jake's bitch. Or at least his cock's bitch. It was hot and deliciously hard, thick but not too much so, pistoning in and out as he kissed her roughly then suckled first at one nipple and then the other. He sweated and grunted and took the Lord's name in vain with hungry abandon as she dragged her nails down his back and thrust her hips up at him, urging him on and on and on. And though she could have ridden the waves far longer than he lasted, she couldn't deny she enjoyed his sudden, hard climax. He arched and groaned, thrusting deep and fast until he roared out his orgasm, still driving into her, then, at last spent, he lay atop her and sloppily kissed her throat and cheek and ear.

For good and ill, Jake turned out to be a one-trick pony, and though she enjoyed his fit, masculine body, she did not want it in bed with her all night. Before he grew too drowsy, she encouraged him to "clean up" in the bathroom. That provided an opportunity to put on her robe—handily hung over a chair before she'd gone out so she'd not have to go into the closet to get it—and lay Jake's clothes out so he could dress, receive a kiss and a hug and be sent on his way. She had an early flight home, she lied, to ensure his ego remained intact. He mumbled something about hoping to see her again sometime, but by then her mind was miles away, or more accurately, in her bedroom closet.

Closing the door behind the guest and turning out the light, Selby took a moment to contemplate what to do next. She was certain she would not open the closet door, but she toyed with the idea of getting into bed and feigning sleep until she actually saw Kate leave. In the end, she opted for a quick shower, and by the time she returned to bed, the closet door was closed.

Months passed before Selby finally did decide to confront Kate, and then she found she couldn't. She was mired in doubt.

She had set up no fewer than six hotel rendezvous since the first, always knowing her almond-eyed Kate would be watching. The irony was not lost on her that the desire to fulfill Kate's voyeuristic needs was driving her to increasingly frequent, and often fabulous, one-time sexual encounters with men. To top off her concerns, there was the real fear that if she did confront Kate, something wonderful would be lost between them. She managed to work herself into a writer's block, the first of her career, increasingly certain their relationship hinged on maintaining their strange status quo.

"What about returning to the Indian Partition idea?" Kate suggested over coffee one morning. Selby knew she meant well, suggesting that she stop trying to force herself to write a book that simply wasn't ready to be written, and try something else. She referred in particular to a sweeping novel of love and betrayal in 1947, as the British pulled out of India after the creation of Pakistan. So much pain and violence as people were forced to leave their homes and friends. Selby meant to personalize it, to tell the tale of lovers separated by faith. "I do love the idea that Meena catches Ashok in bed with Arzu as a way of forcing him to accept the inevitable," Kate encouraged.

Selby sighed, shaking her messy blonde head. "It's so melodramatic." But what she really meant was *It's so fragile*. She had never put a name to her sexual desires. Bisexual was perhaps the most literally accurate, but her pleasure with men was so entirely wrapped up in her pleasure with Kate. Kate, with her thick black hair and her neat, trim body. Kate, with her soft, full lips and small, firm breasts. Her soft climactic whimpers; her eager, devouring mouth. Yet, though no individual man compelled her as Kate did, she enjoyed the harder kisses, the weight of a strong body over hers, the cock pounding inside her. She wanted it all, and she had it all. She and Kate were both content, weren't they? All was perfect but for the nagging doubt over whether the secret of Kate's voyeurism—and Selby's knowledge of it—was acceptable between them.

She drew herself out of her reverie to sneak a glance at Kate while reaching for the cream. Kate was going through some bills with her usual tidy effectiveness. The familiar dark eyes lifted, met hers then drew away. Was there anxiety in their depths? Selby took a deep breath and tried to keep her gaze level. "Kate," she began, then paused when Kate looked up again. "I know."

Kate pressed her lips together tightly, a habit she had when anticipating bad news. Selby knew the expression well from canceled contracts and badly edited interviews. Now, though, the look meant something else. And Selby felt a shudder run through her. They were on the edge of a disclosure that felt like betrayal, and she had no doubt Kate felt the same as she watched her lover's cheeks flush.

Time hung, suspended, crackling with tension that struck Selby as frightening yet simultaneously a bit absurd. She felt as if she'd wandered into one of her novels, or worse, one of the lurid bodice rippers she convinced herself were beneath her. But her heart hammered and an image rose of Kate, stripped roughly bare before her, frantically trying to cover herself, ashamed. She suddenly felt desperately protective, longing to wrap Kate tightly in her arms. Her hand gripped her coffee cup tightly as Kate's eyes widened. She knew without question that the words she was about to speak would transform the beauty of what they shared into something sordid, a dirty little game of hide and seek. It was as if she was watching someone publicly ridicule the woman she loved—and yes, Selby admitted to herself, she did love Kate fiercely—only she was the one doing the ridiculing.

"Yes?" Kate prompted, voice shaky.

Selby swallowed hard. No one would ruin the relationship

between them, the strange status quo that suited them both so wonderfully, especially not Selby herself. "I know," she said at last, "that I'm going to be able to write today."

Kate's glowing smile was more reward than a million-dollar royalty check.

WALKING
THE WALK

Shanna Germain

Black knee-high combat boots, laced up with hot pink. A red miniskirt with a line of lace at the hem that barely covered my thighs. A white lace bra that said SL on one cup and UT on the other in red magic marker.

I swiped a quick splash of crimson across my lips, then stepped back to look at myself in the mirror. Totally, completely exposed. How had I let them convince me this was a good idea? I never even took the garbage out without jeans and a T-shirt.

There was a knock at the bathroom door. "Caroline…" Sammie's soft, cajoling voice came through the wood. "Come on out, Caroline…"

"No," I said. "I can't…" Going out in public in next to nothing was panic-inducing enough; participating in a SlutWalk in little more than a bra and a bit of fabric around my ass was making my heart palpitate so hard I could feel it in my throat.

"Don't make us come in there and get you!" I could hear giggles from the other side of the door. Jason and Sammie both.

Just waiting for me to come out. Vultures.

"Fuck you both," I said. Just because they were all about showing their bodies off all the time, making their views public. I was the quiet, shy door mouse of the three of us, content to stay at home while they went off gallivanting and doing their thing. As long as they came back to me, told me about their exploits and then fucked me into oblivion, I was completely content. I had no need to make myself seen.

"Come on, Caro." This time it was Jason, wheedling. He made little scratching noises against the door with his nails. "We promise to protect you."

"Protect me? From what? You two are the ones I need protection from. Conning me into this..." I sat on the side of the tub, my head in my hands. My cheeks were already pink and hot. The more embarrassed I got, the hotter and pinker they would get.

I could just stay locked in the bathroom forever, sitting on the side of the tub in my bra and combat boots.

But of course, I couldn't. I'd promised them that I'd go to one event with them, their choice, and the bastards had chosen this one.

I opened the door.

"Oh, man," Jason said as soon as I stepped into the living room. He was kneeling outside the door, waiting for me, his hands on his thighs. He has the most beautiful curved cock—we call it Benjamin, "early to bed, early to rise." Already it was hard and bobbing between his legs. I wanted to suck him into my mouth, make him forget this whole crazy idea. "Caro, you should totally dress like that more often."

"I don't think having a guy drool over her is exactly the point of SlutWalk," Sammie said. She was sprawled on the couch, wearing nothing more than a couple of pieces of hot pink duct tape crisscrossed over her nipples. One hand played along the short curls between her legs.

"Sure it is," Jason said. "You like it when I drool over you, don't you, Caro?" He leaned forward and kissed the front of my thigh.

"Aren't you supposed to be dressed anyway, Jas?" I asked, settling a hand softly in his short hair. "I thought it was only the girls that got naked."

He shrugged and looked up at me, a sheepish grin spreading on his face. Any excuse to get naked or mostly naked was good enough for him.

"Right," I said, laughing.

He resumed kissing my legs, trailing his tongue along the inside of one thigh, nipping at my skin. His palm found the curve of my butt and cupped it. "Wait..." he said. "You're wearing panties?"

"Yeah," I said. Of course I was.

He lifted my skirt. I'd worn the most covering panties I owned—my geek boy-cut shorts that said SPEAK FRIEND AND ENTER on the front. I figured it would be funny, and at least semi-concealing, if somehow my skirt got blown up or something.

"Oh, no, no," he said. "That won't do."

"What?"

"Tell her, Sam. Tell her she can't wear panties—especially not full-coverage panties—to a SlutWalk."

"You can't wear panties to a SlutWalk." Sammie was smirking at me from the couch, one hand still tucked between her legs. The other hand began leisurely pulling the duct tape off her nipples, a sure sign that I was in for it.

Jason reached up and tucked his fingers into both sides of my panties and pulled them down over my ass and down to my knees.

"But..." I said.

"Trust me," Jason said.

I started to say something about how there was a lot of "trust me" stuff being tossed around, but then he started brushing his fingers along my labia, in that super-soft way I like best and the words pretty much went out of my head.

He stroked me gently, until I felt myself growing wet, until I couldn't stop myself from pushing against his fingers. He teased like that, making me clench my teeth against the desire. With his other hand, he tugged my panties all the way down.

"Step out of them," Sammie ordered from the couch.

I did my best, my legs wobbly with want, having to put a hand on Jason's shoulder so I wouldn't fall. Jason picked the panties up, brought them to his nose and inhaled long and deep. "Mmm," he said. "I love the way you girls smell when you're all revved up."

Now that my panties were all the way off and Jason had stopped touching me, I felt my heart rev up again, knocking against my chest. I couldn't go out there like this, dripping, the insides of my thighs glistening with want.

"You guys," I said. "I don't think I can do this..."

"Sure you can, baby," Sammie said. "We'll help you, I promise." Her croon would have been reassuring except for the crooked smile that she flashed at Jason.

"I saw that," I said, narrowing my eyes at her.

"Come on, Caroline," she said. "Seriously, you look amazing. You are amazing. What's to fear? Besides, you promised."

I sidestepped Jason, who gave a little whine of protest, then plunked myself down on the couch to lean against Sammie's long legs. "I know," I said. "I'm just super nervous. I'm not like you guys."

"I know," Sammie said. She reached out and pulled me

closer to her. "And you don't have to be like us. It's just for fun. Everyone else will be naked, too."

"Meep," I said. It was my old safeword, one we no longer used for fucking, but which often came out of my mouth in times of distress.

"Aw, poor Caroline," Sammie said, tucking one hand into the SL side of my SL-UT bra. Her fingers found my nipple and tweaked it lightly, then rolled it between them until she could get a good grip. When she pinched it, I squeaked then gave a soft moan.

"See?" Sammie whispered. She tucked her face into the side of my neck, gently biting her way up to the edge of my ear. "Come and help me make her feel better, Jason."

Sammie kissed me then, the way I loved best. The hard kind of kiss that captures all of your breath and makes you feel like you're drowning in want. She had one hand at the back of my neck, holding me into it. The other hand still rolled and pinched my nipple. I groaned against her open lips, meeting her tongue with my own, unable to resist.

Jason must have slipped across the room while we were kissing, because suddenly I could feel his hands parting my thighs, his breath warm against my skin. He spread my labia with his fingers and then touched his tongue, just the tip, just a touch, to the point of my clit. Once and again, dabbing at me. Not so soft that it tickled, but not hard enough that it satisfied the ache that was rising up in me.

It sent shudders up me, shudders that Sammie met and quelled with her tongue against mine. I wanted to wiggle away, to groan and arch, but Sammie held me tight with her hands and mouth, and Jason with his lapping, teasing tongue.

"Bastards," I muttered through my groans, and they both laughed. Jason's giggle erupted from between my thighs so hard that it did tickle.

"You love it," Sammie said.

"I do," I agreed. "Kiss me again?"

"I don't think so," she said, eyeing me and then Jason. "Let's switch spots," she said to him.

They didn't actually switch spots; they just maneuvered me to suit their needs, laying me down on the couch so that Jason's mouth met mine, his fingers seeking out my nipples beneath the bra. He kissed totally differently than Sammie, asking for instead of taking, making me reach out for him with my lips, my tongue.

Sammie's fingers opened me, teased my already wet spaces and then slipped wet and slippery inside me. She scissored them lightly, sending me arching up off the couch, forcing me to break the kiss with Jason so I could gasp my pleasure. Sammie grinned wickedly at me, toying with me, her fingers spreading me wide. She sat up on her knees and moved closer so I could reach out and touch her; so I could feel her wet center with my own fingers. I found her clit—the hard, wet point of it—and caught it between my fingertips.

"Jason, too," she said, her voice rough with want.

I reached for Jason with my other hand, found the hard curve of his cock already straining up for my touch. The tip was coated already, and I rubbed my thumb along the moisture before curling my hand around his length.

He groaned, a low-throated sound that sent shivers through me.

"Mouth," Sammie said.

I turned my head, craning for his cock. Jason stood, leaning over me to give me better access. I ran my tongue around the glistening head, brushed my lips over his skin until he groaned. When he pushed against me, I opened my lips, let him sink the wet head into my mouth. I loved the feel of sucking him, taking him deep while Sammie toyed with my clit, rubbing faster and faster, even as she bucked against my hand.

"Going to come be a dirty slut with us?" Sammie's voice was thick with want, almost panting as she stroked her fingers across my clit. Teasing. Always teasing. "Going to strut down the street without your panties?"

I shook my head around Jason's cock, groaning against his length.

"The longer you resist, the worse it's going to be." Sammie pulled away, making me groan again. Then her fingers came down in a slap against my clit. I squealed, pulling back from Jason's cock, my hips arching up automatically into her touch.

"Please," I begged. "Please please please…"

"Say, 'I'm coming to the SlutWalk,'" Sammie said. "'Because I'm your dirty slut.'"

"No…" I groaned. I didn't want to come that badly. I didn't. I'd just wait until they were gone and take my fingers to my own…

And then I could feel Sammie coming against my hand, arching her body into my fingers, coating my skin. Beside me, Jason put his hand on his cock, stroked it fast. I cried out, just from watching and feeling the two of them.

"Say it," Sammie said, fingers thrusting inside me, thumb moving round and round and round on my clit. Jason's hand stroked his cock. I turned and sucked him deep into my mouth so I wouldn't have to say it, so she'd let me come without forcing me to agree.

Sammie said something that I barely heard, taking her fingers from me, and then Jason was pulling himself away from my mouth. I whimpered in want.

"Sorry," he said, in a way that showed he wasn't sorry at all.

They slid me sideways on the couch, angling me so that I

was leaning on the back, my legs up on Jason's shoulders. Jason leaned over me, his cock sliding into me. He was trying to go slow, I could tell, but I was so wet that he couldn't hold back, and he was quickly buried in me all the way with a low groan of want. Sammie's cool fingers found my clit; she leaned so that her nipple was against my lips. I opened my mouth, trying to suck the erect flesh, but she deftly kept it just out of reach, laughing. I was so close that I felt the orgasm riding up through my stomach, tightening my throat.

"All you have to do..." Sammie whispered, licking my nipple between words, her fingers still slapping my clit in time to Jason's thrusts, "...is say yes."

"Yes," I said. "Yes."

"Yes, what?" Sammie asked.

"Yes, I'll...go to your stupid SlutWalk..."

"Without...?"

"Without my panties. Just, please, please..."

Sammie bit my nipple, a tight grip that sent shudders through me. Her fingers tight on my clit and Jason slamming into me, the sound of both their groaned breaths, all of it finally sent the orgasm through me, a shameless shuddering cry releasing from my mouth. I arched off the couch, into Jason's thrusts and Sammie's slaps, my hands reaching for both of them at the same time.

I said a lot of words, most of them nonsense, as the orgasm rode through me and then subsided. The sound of all of us panting made me start to laugh.

"Oh, funny girl now, are you?" Sammie asked. But she was grinning too hard to put on her domme face. Jason, seemingly as spent as I was, pulled himself from between my legs, landing back on the floor with a huff of breath, resting his head against my knee.

I nodded.

"Well," she said. "Let's see how funny you are when you're shaking your bare ass at the SlutWalk."

"We're still doing that?" I asked.

She gave me that look, the one she always gives me when I'm about to get myself in trouble.

"Meep?" I said.

"Come on, Caro," Jason said. "You made a deal."

"Fine, fine," I said. And, suddenly, it was. My body was relaxed, my brain had shut off its typical worrying. So what if I was going to walk mostly naked with a bunch of people looking at me? I had two people who adored me no matter what. I could do this, as long as they were both by my side.

A few hours later, we were hand in hand in hand, traipsing down the street with thousands of other mostly naked people. Jason was wearing my SPEAK FRIEND AND ENTER panties, which didn't even begin to cover any part of him that mattered. Sammie had opted for her hot-pink duct-tape nipple covers. And me? I was wearing nothing but combat boots and a smile big enough for everyone to see.

RE*GRET*ABLE CIRCUMSTANCES

Lane

I should have known when my friend Tallulah said she was hosting a party at Windows to celebrate the war victory, that all of the Hollywood luminaries would be in attendance, including a certain woman I didn't care to see. The number of casualties was staggering on all sides, but the United States and her Allies had finally succeeded in bringing the murderous campaign of Nazi Germany and the rest of the Axis forces to a screeching halt. What better way to celebrate such a decisive triumph than to spend the night dancing and toasting the courage of our boys?

As the lights and bustle of New York City gradually dissolved into the peaceful hamlet of Bedford Village, I twisted my fingers in my lap, racked by the same questions I'd been asking myself since I left my apartment. What the hell was I doing? There was a reason why I spent my entire career avoiding parties. I hated the excessive noise, the constant gossip and the questionable company. So why hadn't I declined Tallulah's invitation in favor of a peaceful evening at home with my cats?

My regret was interrupted by the muffled crooning of jazz instruments. When the taxi turned a corner, Tallulah's mansion, situated on an eminence and distinctive for its innumerable windows, came into view. I paid the driver, opened the door, and a warm breeze flirted with the hem of my dress. The taxi flashed its lights and sped off into the balmy night, leaving me to my own defenses. I sighed, looked up at the house and braced myself for god knew what.

A long row of cars were parked across the street, and I moved past the four black convertibles sitting in the driveway with all the enthusiasm of a pallbearer. My jaw went slack at a naked couple kissing in one of the bedrooms upstairs, indifferent to the parted curtains. There was a gravel path that led to the front door, and I was all but tackled to the ground by a cackling flash of diamonds and red satin. As Tallulah and I moved through the foyer, I saw a former costar in a heated altercation with a gentleman leaning against a bookcase. They both paused to look at me.

"How are you, Greta darling?" Tallulah cupped my face. "You look divine in that dress! It gives you a bit of cleavage."

"Thank you, Tallulah. I like your dress, too."

"Ha! I haven't worn this old thing in years! It was in the back of my wardrobe collecting dust so I thought I'd drag it out for the occasion. It's not every day that we win a war now, is it?"

As Tallulah rambled on about the history of the dress, one of the straps slipped down her shoulder, revealing most of her right breast. Either she genuinely didn't notice or didn't care, and I was more inclined to believe the latter. I cleared my throat and tried not to stare when she casually pulled up the strap, as if she were plucking a piece of lint from a sweater. She stuck her head into the cocktail lounge and called for her servant, who was watching a man snort something off a compact mirror. Tallulah tossed back her head in manic laughter, inspiring the curious glances of those nearby.

"Lillian darling, all the cocaine in the world won't make him sleep with you. Believe me, I've tried. Now please take Greta's coat to the closet for her."

"Yes, Miss Tallulah!"

The young woman stumbled into the foyer with her arms outstretched and smiled at me. Her eyes were dilated, there was a ring of white in her left nostril and her breath reeked of hard liquor, bourbon or whiskey, perhaps. I reluctantly gave her my coat, and hoped that it wouldn't get sprayed with something undesirable en route to the closet.

A crystal chandelier presided over a stunning aggregation of suits and gowns and the air was pungent with cigarette smoke, perfume and alcohol. The lounge echoed with spirited conversation and laughter and I watched a group of men snap their fingers and tap their feet in time to a lively tune played by the four musicians at the center. As if on cue, a flock of actors, producers, directors and strangers charged at me, and I froze at the flurry of comments and questions concerning my early retirement. After the failure of my last film, I had no intention of ever acting again.

"She'll be back!" Tallulah asserted, taking a glass of champagne from the butler.

"Oh, darlings, it feels so good to be off the wagon! I don't know what I'd have done if I had to wait another fucking day! But we did it! We won!"

A deafening roar of approval followed and our hostess pumped her glass high into the air, causing its bubbling contents to spill down her arm. The croak of the trumpet tore through the shouts and applause, the crowd dispersed, and Tallulah danced a wild swing with Joan Crawford.

The butler approached me with his champagne tray and I took a glass, along with two crabmeat canapés from the hors d'oeuvres table. I ate one, waited for a couple to spin past, then moved across the room to sit on a settee, opposite a fat woman who was rummaging through her bag. As I ate the second canapé, she paused to gawk as if she could suddenly see after a lifetime of blindness.

"The gloomy Swede at a Tallulah party, eh?" Her coarse Brooklyn accent and cloying perfume made me cringe. "Fancy that! I'm sure I've got one in this fucking bag somewhere, but would you happen to have a light?"

I took one out of my purse and lit her cigarette. The woman took a sharp drag and fell back against the cushions, the corners of her blood-red lips twitching in a deranged smile. She took the cigarette out of her mouth, muttered something unintelligible, then shuffled away without so much as a thank-you. I lit my own cigarette, grateful for the solitude while I had it.

The musicians concluded their number and a peal of laughter carried over the fading cheers. By some terrible luck, I turned toward the fireplace and there *she* was, wearing a gown that clung to her body like a shimmering coat of gold paint, and split at the sides to reveal her elegant legs. Her blonde hair was swept into a loose chignon and she wore pearls in her ears and around her throat. Through the haze of smoke it looked like a dream, but the knot in my stomach that formed as she kissed another woman was very much real.

I'd been on the receiving end of such attention years before I'd come to America. Before the war, Berlin was a popular hub for deviant lifestyles of all sorts. I was a shy, awkward teenager and Marlene was a cabaret performer with an air of worldliness and sophistication. One evening, as she strutted across the stage in a risqué act, she spotted me sitting in the audience, plucked a violet from her garter and tossed it onto my table, much to the amusement of everyone. When the show concluded, Marlene whisked me off to her hotel suite in Wilmersdorf where she introduced me to the world of lesbian sex.

I reclined nude on a canopied bed of crisp white linens and damask cushions, my arm slung over the mattress, watching the orange flames jump and shimmy in the fireplace. Clothes and shoes were scattered across the floor and the furniture, and a breeze swept through the window, engaging the candles lined up across the mantelpiece in a rhythmic dance. Their little shadows skipped and leapt across the wallpaper, and my head lolled languidly to one side as I basked in a haven of luxury beyond my wildest dreams.

Amid billowing clouds of steam, Marlene emerged from the bathroom, dressed in a robe that clung to the soft curves of her breasts and thighs. I sat up as the garment melted into a puddle at her feet, and she crawled across the bed on all fours, coaxing me to lie on my back again. She took my face in her hands and I could taste the cognac on her lips. I pulled her over me, so that her sex was aligned with mine, and she smiled.

I arched my breasts into her palms as she pinched my nipples then licked her way down my body till her face was level with my waist. My legs fell open of their own accord, exposing my tight sex to the warmth of her breath. Marlene kissed the lips gently, spread them apart and licked my clitoris with the tip of her tongue. When she began to suck with firm, but gentle pressure, liquid heat built deep in my core and the sensation of moist flesh against moist flesh made me writhe and grind against her face. I held her head down and those lips vibrated in a low, taunting chuckle.

"You want me to make you come, susse?"

"Yes..." I whispered. "Please..."

"Damn it, Greta! Watch the ash on my new rug!"

I shook my head and frowned at the little black spot on the burgundy and gold pattern. The ashtray on the table had completely escaped my notice and I apologized to Tallulah, who had a wry smirk on her face. I blinked as Joan skipped over to us, her large eyes jubilant.

"There you are!" Tallulah laughed. "What the hell were you doing in the bathroom that long?"

"Wouldn't you like to know?" Joan winked at me. "Miss Greta, your hair is fabulous. Really, you should wear it that way more often."

I thanked her, though my hair hung straight and just above my shoulders as it always did.

"Now," Joan held out her hand to Tallulah as the band struck up a new tune. "Shall we continue?"

I closed my eyes and realized I couldn't stay in this madhouse any longer. When Tallulah and Joan were gone, I put out my cigarette, left my glass on the table, and left the lounge, ignoring the stares and remarks all around. I recalled a taxi station during the drive, which couldn't have been more than ten or fifteen minutes away, and darkness be damned, I was a fast walker.

When I reached the front door, a little dog ran up and her earsplitting bark made everyone in the foyer look at me. Tallulah appeared, holding my glass and pouting.

"You could've finished the champagne, at least! Do you think this shit is cheap?" She drank it herself, advanced toward me and softened her tone. "Darling, I'm sorry, you don't have to go. Please," she reached out and brushed my wrist, "I think we need to talk."

At the opposite end of the foyer was a set of French doors

that led to the patio. Its tables and chairs overlooked the garden, cloaked in darkness except for the muted glow of the swimming pool. Tallulah paused to light a marijuana cigarette then so closely skirted the edge of the pool that I expected her to fall in. We lay together in her hammock, smoking and watching the stars peeking through the tree branches.

"So, Tallulah," I tried to sound as detached as possible. "Have you seen Marlene's pretty new toy?"

"Of course I have darling, it's my party! She's Margaret, the daughter of a producer I know. She's just a temporary diversion, though. You're a much better fit for Marlene's palate."

"I don't want her."

"Oh? Then I suppose the orgasmic look you had on your face when you were staring at her was a figment of my imagination." She snickered. "Let's not, darling, all right? I've known you both too long."

Tallulah's impish grin was that of a friend who could see past the façade, though it was a little unsettling just how much she knew about everyone and everything. I shook my head when she offered me the rest of the cigarette, and after a few more drags, she flicked it away. My scalp prickled when she slid her hand over mine.

"I was thinking about our first formal meeting. You remember that, don't you?"

"Yes, at Salka's house." I enjoyed the warm tingling coursing through my fingers and toes. "You pulled my eyelashes to see if they were real."

"Well, yes, but after that." Tallulah's hair cascaded into her face, but it didn't obscure the glint in her blue eyes. "We played tennis all afternoon, had a few drinks and then we..."

Her lips felt full, warm, soft. She rolled out of the hammock and gestured for me to follow. We darted like shadows past the

patio and entered the mansion through a side door. It opened to
a room the size of a closet, redolent of bourbon and cigarettes,
and it was packed to the ceiling with magazines, books, and
antiques. Beyond the mountains of junk was a private flight of
stairs. When we reached the second floor, Tallulah seized my
waist and we kissed again with more abandon.

She nudged open the door to the master bedroom and closed
it behind us. I was about to remark on the charming simplicity
of the décor when my bag dropped to the floor with a thud. A
nude Marlene crawled toward the foot of the bed, wrapped her
arms around one of the posts and batted her eyelashes at us. I
glared at Tallulah, who acted like this was of no consequence.
She tossed her clothes and heels aside and tackled Marlene to the
mattress. The déjà vu was too much and as they rolled around
like reunited lovers, I stood there like a fool. If this was their
idea of a prank, I didn't find it at all funny.

"Tallulah, thank you for your hospitality, but I'm really
going to have to leave now."

It took herculean effort for me to pull myself away, but I
managed to grab the doorknob. A hand firmly closed over mine,
and that honey-velvet purr in my ear made the backs of my knees
turn to water.

"You know you want to play with us, *susse.*"

I pivoted and fixed Marlene with a look of derision, but
before I could even try to put her in her place, she pulled down
the straps of my dress, fingers like butterfly wings over my skin.
My head fell back against the door as she cupped my breasts,
and swirled her tongue over my erect nipples. I groaned in
spite of myself and tilted her head up to look at her face. The
broad forehead, hooded eyes and sculpted cheekbones were as
alluring as ever, and that cupid's bow of a mouth was painted a
rich red.

"You'll remember this, I'm sure," Marlene murmured with a quick kiss.

She swept to the bedside where Tallulah was sitting with her fingers nestled between her thighs. I pressed my back against the door as Marlene dropped, pushed Tallulah's hand aside and buried her face between her legs. I thumbed my nipples in time with Tallulah's moans, feeling my own sex ripen in anticipation. Her eyes met mine, wide and pleading, and it was as though our bodies were attuned to the same sensations. Soon, Tallulah fell back on her elbows, breathless and spent.

"Shit!" She gasped. "You haven't changed, Marlene. Just like old times!" I raised my eyebrow and felt, what was it? A stab of jealousy? It seemed there was no actress in Hollywood immune to Marlene's charms. Grinning, she climbed next to Tallulah and propped herself against the stack of pillows. Both women looked at me, and Marlene ran her fingers over the fine, damp foliage of hair between her legs. She bit her lip and circled her clitoris, then spread her labia apart, exposing the pink, puckered hole. I panted as Marlene put out her hand for Tallulah to taste, then resumed, blue eyes flickering, but always fixed in my direction.

"Take off the rest of your clothes and come here, *liebe*," Marlene ordered between clenched teeth, splaying her legs wider. I climbed onto the bed, kissed where her thigh met her pelvis, then dipped a finger into her sex to feel how moist she was. With the same finger, I brushed her little hood and the nub under it, changing my cadence so that she never knew what to expect. Her breaths came ragged as my tongue pried her open to lap up the smoky fluid that coated her inner lips. I thrust in and out, her hands knotted in my hair, and her sex clamped around me for the last time.

"Yes, *liebe*!" Marlene found her voice and cried out again

and again. I sat up on my hands and knees, face coated in her juices and gloated. In her vulnerable state, she looked especially lovely.

"What a nice, firm ass you have, Greta," Tallulah smacked it hard till a hot flush spread over the cheeks. My eyes watered, the sting was new to me, but I liked it. She pulled me up so that I was up on my knees and leaning back against her, then played with my breasts. She offered them to Marlene, who grazed my nipples with her teeth, while running her hands over the rest of my body. My every fiber was burning, and I didn't know what to do with myself as a flurry of smooth hands rubbed, prodded, stroked, massaged and did all manner of pleasurable things to me.

"Please," I begged, my ability to express myself reduced to breathless words rather than complete thoughts. I looked down as Marlene cupped my sex, but refrained from sliding a finger inside. My hands balled into fists, "I need...I want...please..."

"Hmm," Tallulah kissed my ear and when she felt the spot between my sex and my anus, my thighs trembled at the novel sensation. "You're going to get what you want darling, it's only fair. What do you say, Marlene?"

"But of course." The German beauty nipped my collarbone, caressed the small of my back and smiled at Tallulah over my shoulder. "I think," she pinched and rolled the lips of my sex over my clitoris, "that you should taste her, Tallulah. And be creative, by all means."

They whispered and chuckled some more, but I was only able to catch fragments of it as I drifted away into blissful delirium. I was brought back to reality when Tallulah maneuvered herself under me so that her face was between my legs. She instructed me to stay up on my knees while she probed the spongy region deep at my core. Those cool, smooth, hard knuckles felt exquisite and I clamped down on her fingers, desperate to keep them lodged where they were. I worked my hips in circles, but before I knew it, Tallulah pulled her hand away and eased me down onto her mouth.

"Oh, god!" I screamed, no longer myself. My hips immediately undulated, then stilled when Tallulah grabbed me firmly to limit my movements. My sex spread over her lips and tongue, and as Tallulah slurped loudly, Marlene pressed her breasts to mine and reached around to squeeze my bottom with both hands. Her mouth was wet and insistent over my feverish face and neck, and pleasure lanced through me as she hooked a finger just under my clitoris in an agonizingly slow come-hither motion.

"You like that don't you, *liebe*?" She asked. "Tell me...tell me..."

Lost for words, I crushed my mouth to hers in reply; tongues probing, pushing and exploring as our sweaty bodies swayed together. Marlene strummed my clitoris, and digging my knees into the sheets on either side of Tallulah's head, I worked my aching sex as much as I could over her talented mouth. I heard her muffled groan of assent as she held me down hard on her, inhaling me, drinking me, sucking me, while Marlene picked up a faster pace on my clitoris. I whimpered into her mouth, tottering on the brink, till at last, hot ripples shot out from my womb and flooded my limbs. Both women kept at what they were doing and I arched sharply, cries rising to the ceiling, coming over and over till they were satisfied. As the waves ebbed, I rolled onto my side, enveloped in my white-heat nirvana.

For a time, it could have been seconds, minutes or hours, we lay together, a heap of arms and legs tangled over scattered pillows and disheveled sheets. Marlene kissed my ear and said something about loving me, but I was too preoccupied with trying to make sense of what the hell just happened. I looked at

Tallulah, who moved to the ottoman in front of her vanity. She pulled open her drawers, and bottles of nail polish, hairspray and foundation went flying till at last she found what she was looking for.

"Thank god for Elizabeth Arden!" Tallulah applied the lipstick, evened it with her finger, then hastily ran a brush through her hair, while watching Marlene and me in her mirror. "Without this stuff my face looks pale as a goddamn sheet, and it would be impolite to give anybody a heart attack." She paused to wink at my reflection. "But oh, Greta, darling! You do indeed have a delightful little cunt." Her purr made my sex pulse all over again, and I gave myself away by squeezing my thighs together. Tallulah breezed out of the room without bothering to put on a robe. I could hear her singing, or more like croaking the words to a Billie Holiday song as she went down the hallway. I shook my head and chuckled at the absurdity of all of this. But Marlene was frowning.

"*Liebe*?" She whispered. "Don't you have anything to say?"

I wished she would stop calling me that; it was almost as irritating as Tallulah's endearment of choice. Marlene put her arm around me, but I abruptly pulled away and sat at the vanity. Amid the mess of beauty products was a box of Craven A cigarettes and some matches. I blew smoke at the German's stunned, but determined reflection. She asked me to pass her a cigarette, so I turned and hurled the box at her, sending several of the white sticks sailing. Marlene's lips pressed into a tight line and she launched herself at me, throwing her arms around my shoulders.

"I know what you're trying to do, Greta." Her mouth was hot and slick on my ear. "It's been your tactic of choice for years whenever someone gets too close." Her fingers traced my collarbone then slid down to the swells of my breasts and I cursed myself for trembling. "But when I truly love somebody, I'm not easily dissuaded, though you do try my patience."

Marlene stole my cigarette and slid it erotically between her lips. She tossed her head back and blew out the smoke in perfect O's that dissipated in the air. With a kiss on my cheek, she stuck the cigarette into my startled mouth and flung herself onto the chaise lounge with a melodious sigh.

I crushed out the cigarette and rubbed my temples. I knew that I was incapable of loving anybody, but just watching Marlene on her back, clutching a cushion and softly humming at the ceiling, filled my frigid heart with something that was too close to love for my comfort. I wanted her and I reviled her, and my inability to wrap my head around this contradiction made me sink my nails into my palms in sheer despair and frustration.

"When you love *somebody*?" I repeated, incredulous. I tried to blot the fireplace kiss from my mind. "You've had more bed partners than most people, so why should I believe that I'm more than just another conquest?"

"Going to bed with somebody isn't synonymous with loving them," Marlene countered sharply. "You and I did more in Europe than have sex. You just have a very selective memory. I wanted to spend my life with you, but you turned your back on *me*. You're afraid, Greta. Afraid and insecure."

"God almighty!" Tallulah tumbled into the room, still naked, holding a bottle of champagne in one hand and three glasses in the other. Marlene relieved her of the glasses and Tallulah collapsed onto the chaise lounge with her arm draped dramatically over her head. "It's madness down there, darlings," she moaned, though she didn't really seem too upset. "If they're not stumbling around drunk, they're swinging from the chandeliers. Do you know, I was going down the stairs and almost fell on my ass in a pool of vomit?" She stuck a corkscrew into the champagne bottle and twisted it. "I looked for Lillian and guess where that tart was? Out on the patio with her face down in Harold's lap!"

"I thought he was gay?" Marlene set the glasses on the little table before them.

"He is! But when you're high, I suppose it doesn't matter who's sucking your cock." Tallulah shrugged and poured out the champagne. "I left them to their fun and mopped up the mess myself."

I wasn't sure if Tallulah was genuinely oblivious to the hostility in the air, or was just using her humor to diffuse it. I moved from the vanity, Marlene and I reached for the same glass, and when our hands made contact, I rebounded like water on a hot surface. She glared at me as I sat on the adjacent armchair and swallowed half of the sweet liquid, a welcome relief for my dry throat.

I pointedly asked if Tallulah told anyone about our ménage à trois.

"Of course not, darling, it's our little secret." She tapped her teeth against the rim of her glass then scowled. "Are those my Craven A's on the floor?" Apologizing, I put them back in the box without detailing what happened. I gave them to her, returned to my seat, and stared at the bed, while Marlene inspected her nails.

There was silence until Tallulah cleared her throat and asked if we'd made any progress putting our feud to rest.

"*I* want to," Marlene insisted. "There are just so many... impediments." I studied her facial movements: a twitch of the arched brows, a subtle flare of the nostrils, a brief flash of perfect white teeth. All the while those eyes were on me, a gaze of fire that I matched with pure ice. It was as if we were locked in a perpetual stalemate, with neither of us willing or able to budge. We knew that there was something between us, but there wasn't a name for it and there didn't need to be. After tonight, we would go our separate ways for another several years or so, only to inevitably cross paths again in another state or perhaps another country.

It was, in truth, the only feasible arrangement.

RIGHT-RED FLAGGING

Sinclair Sexsmith

Every Tuesday night the local boy bar is transformed into a leather cruising night, and I go every chance I get. It's no stretch for my queer identity, not even a stretch for my dyke one—these days, fucking a cis guy is the queerest act there is. Me, I prefer the gay boys, the leather daddies, the twinks, the trans fags; so much more no-nonsense than the straight guys, though I'll admit to the occasional foray into swinging. The straight picket-fence husband and his SUV-driving wife think they get to do a little girl-swap for my sweetie, but in fact we go homo and put the girls together, leaving me with him. He's eager to bend over for my cock after we watch them go at it for a while, and inevitably all too eager to follow up with me after. They don't have to wonder if they're gay this way, though I make certain to assure them that they are, just to fuck with 'em.

The leather fags are different. No identity crisis, no curiosity or treating me like a circus sideshow act, no awkward gender questions or homophobia couched in ignorance. Especially when I'm in drag.

Passing is a challenge, but after many consults with my drag king buddy and many trial-and-error accidents, I have the formula down. Nothing superfluous, as few props and costumes as possible.

Dark tight jeans, a jock to arrange my package, no undies. Chaps, sometimes. My chest binder, full-torso length, because it's hard to hide my tits, but worth it. T-shirt from one of the leather fests if I'm trying to draw attention and get fucked, a plain black one if I want to do the fucking. My hair just so. Sometimes a five o'clock shadow is a nice touch, but in the dark bar, who can see it anyway?

The one single earring is a key accessory. Then it's either the leather wrist cuff with an O-ring; the plain, heavy belt buckle; or leather suspenders, depending on my mood. If it's cold, a leather jacket. The one with the cock rings in the epaulets.

I don't know what it is about this combination, maybe I could wear anything now that I've been doing it awhile, maybe I've adapted the energy and it is no longer about the clothes, but this is what works, so I stick with it. Hell, maybe I don't pass at all and the boys either know I'm in drag or think I'm a trans guy who isn't taking T—either way, they don't seem to care.

Sometimes my friends come with me—you'd be surprised how useful a dyke wingman is in a boy bar. Especially for the ones who aren't on the prowl. But since Kelli got picked up by those two trans fags and I spent the night at the bar drinking too much whiskey, I've gone at it on my own more often. My friends don't seem to care that I get a craving for dick and go for it. They don't see me as any less queer, just as perhaps differently queer than they are. None of us use the word *bisexual,* though perhaps that is the most fitting. Seems like we all went through that phase before we came out as full-on gay...for me, it just wasn't a phase.

Tonight, I see him as soon as I enter the room, eyes adjusting to the darkness that still feels full of cigarette smoke, even though it's no longer legal to smoke indoors, and he sees me. He's at the bar sucking on a long-neck beer, wearing a snap-down, worn-through cowboy shirt and jeans, and we make eye contact. In gay-boy world, that means we might as well have been dating for three years and just walked into the hotel room after our prom. I order a beer, too, and wait at the curve of the bar.

He watches me while not looking like he's watching me. I notice a red hanky in his back right pocket and as he brings the beer up to his mouth for the last swig, I slip off my bar stool and make my way toward the back hallway, the bathrooms and the door to the back patio. I lean against the wall in a dark patch of the path, thumbs hooked into my belt loops. He follows a moment later, sauntering slowly into the hall, and stops, seeing me.

"Hi," I say. He grins, a crooked half smirk that darkens his already deep-set eyes. He's more plump than muscular but still has a good shape, firm and solid.

"Hi," he says.

"So," I say. He waits. I curl my finger without moving my hand from my hip, and he takes a few steps toward me. I can't tell who he thinks I am or what he thinks I expect, but he seems willing to find out. When he is just a foot or two from me, and I can smell his sweat and make out the stubble on his chin, I reach out for his upper arm and grip it. "Are you going to kiss me, or what?"

That smile comes back, the cocky half grin, and he looks almost shy for a second. It is perhaps an intimate act to request, but I like it. And here, under this disguise, in this bar, on this night, I go for what I want. He leans in and I keep his body at a distance with my grip, let him reach for me with his mouth, watch as he swallows and licks his lips and swallows again. He backs off, comes toward me again, and I play with the distance between us, letting the tension build as I feel his arms flex and feet fumble. Finally, I lighten my grip and our lips crash into each other, eager and hungry and devouring.

He brings his arms up around my neck even though I'm a good four inches shorter than him, or maybe because of it. I trail my hands down to his hips and they rest easily as we explore each other's mouth. His tongue is alternately hard and soft, subtle and insistent. I take a handful of his ass and he groans.

He pulls back just far enough to form words. "My place is two blocks away."

"Yes, please."

We break and I follow him to the door. On the way there, he mutters his name, which I promptly forget. I wonder if it's his real name. I wonder which name I should give him, but before I respond he says something about Tuesday being his favorite night of the week and we're at the door to his apartment, so I don't ever offer my name. He goes first and holds the door back for me, leads me up some plain narrow stairs. Inside, it's a studio that is sparse and disheveled, and we're kissing again before the door is even closed.

He bites at my neck, sucks on my earlobe and I soften, my shoulders relaxing, my cock getting harder. I feel his shaft through the front of his jeans and he's hard, straining against his zipper.

I pull the hanky out of his back pocket. "Red, huh?"

He nods, head low again as he bites my shoulder through my T-shirt. *Fuck, yes.* I catch his mouth with mine and suck, pull him by the belt across his tiny kitchen, around the fairly large ficus tree, over to the bed under the one huge window. It must get a lot of light; he's got a lot of healthy-looking, dark-green growing things that I identify only as "houseplants."

I sit on the bed and pull his hips in front of me, working his belt off with my hands as I shove my mouth at his cock through his jeans. He's not wearing any underwear. I can feel it jump a little, tense and pulse, can feel the heat of it through the thick fabric. He closes his eyes, rolls his head back, opens them and watches me. I bite at the shaft through his jeans as I get the buckle and his jeans undone, unzipped. I suck the spit back that has gathered into my mouth and swallow. He reaches into his back pocket and hands me a condom, then brings his cock out of his jeans.

It looks like mine, kind of—the strap-on that is my favorite, I mean. Decent length and a little bit of girth, but still slender enough to go easily down throats. It's not as neat, though—it has an up curve where mine is just straight, and the skin at the base is more wrinkled. Bodies are messy. He smells sour and like sweat. I'm a little fascinated, and realize I'm staring, one hand on the condom in my lap and one hand on his thigh, as a few drops of precome slide down the shaft.

I feel sheepish, like I'm caught, and don't look up at him as I tear the package open and roll it down onto his dick. Unlubricated. Nice. Gay boys are so smart with their prophylactics.

It's a cock, not a strap-on, and I don't care how I look sucking it, I just care how he feels it, and how I feel it, getting my mouth filled up and fed in a primal, nourishing way. So I slide the head of his cock into my mouth and hold it there a moment, not quite feeling the blood in his skin through the condom but definitely aware of the heat, before I swallow the whole thing. I want to take more of it than I can and when it hits my throat, I almost gag before I slide it back out, my eyes watering. His hips shudder forward and I work it back in slower, close my lips tight around his shaft, close my eyes and feel myself drinking him down.

"Ohhh, fuck," he breathes out, low. His pubic hair is trimmed though not shaved, short and dark to match the hair on his head and the fur he's got on his arms. I finger his balls, shift them in the palm of my hand before letting my finger rest behind them and feeling his ass respond like I've hit a button.

I *mmm* with his cock in my mouth and the reverberations give him a chill; his body wriggles from the base of his spine up his back. I keep his cock in my mouth, sucking and teasing with my tongue, and let my hand wander farther toward his asshole.

I lick his shaft before taking it out of my mouth. "Got any gloves?" I say.

He shakes his head. "No. Sorry."

"Lube?"

"Yeah." I move my hand and he shifts to the bedside table to retrieve a pump bottle hiding under a plant with long skinny leaves. It wasn't cold tonight, so I have no jacket, but I did manage to stuff my tiny safer-sex supply kit into my back pocket. I take out one of the two smashed black gloves (hey, you never know) and replace the condom and other glove in my jeans. Does the black glove give away that I'm a dyke? Do gay boys ever carry the black ones? I don't know who he thinks I am, but it's clear he's going to let me play, and that's what matters.

He's kicked off his shoes and slid his jeans down over his legs into a pile on the floor. I stand and move next to him on the side of the bed, grab his lapels and unsnap his plaid cowboy shirt, leaving it on and open, then kiss him again and take the lube bottle from his hand. "Thanks."

I tilt my head toward the bed and he sits. I push his chest back and go for his cock again, catching it with my lips, kissing the tip, before sliding it deeper into my mouth. I can't get it all the way down, but I keep trying. He opens his knees a little and puts one foot flat on the bed. I work the lube onto my gloved hand while his dick is still in my mouth and bring my hand under him to slide my fingers along his crack. He's smooth and sensitive, moving his head to the side and pressing the inside of his arm at his mouth as he pushes at the wall with his hand then grips the windowsill. It's cute. Submissive, even, in an uncomplicated way that indicates he's just feeling it, not thinking about it. I circle his asshole with my fingertip while I keep sucking, and when his hips come up off the bed and he starts pushing against my hand and fingers, I let him press down onto it and slip in one finger to the knuckle. He groans immediately, a relief and a turn-on, and his cock twitches from the base again. I slide the whole finger in and out and he's open and eager.

"More," he manages, almost a question, almost a demand.

I add another, then two, and he isn't fazed, keeps gyrating on my hand. I slide his dick out of my mouth and prop myself back on my elbows to get a better angle, and add another finger. It slides in so easily. Fucking an asshole is so different than pussy. I've got four fingers inside him before I know it, and his breathing has deepened, coming in thick exhales from his belly. His shirt is tangled under his arms and falling open over his stomach and chest. I can see his nipples, hard, through his wisps of dark chest hair. I look up at him and we make eye contact, his eyes playful and pleading, and I pool more lube into the palm of my hand, let it drip down inside him, and coat the outside with as much as I can reach. There's a growing wet spot on his plain dark blue bedspread underneath my hand. He nods a little when I push, groans.

"Yeah," he mutters, "yeah, yeah..." and I'm in, my whole hand, past my thumb to the wrist. There's no cervix to hit and my fingers aren't as cramped, but long, smashed together at the width rather than length. His body bucks a little and quiets when I move my hand, and I can feel him pulsing around my fingers, palm, wrist.

He has both his arms up, hands gripping the windowsill, and both of his knees up, feet flat on the bed. When his body calms a bit more I make a few tiny movements with my hand, and he moans immediately. I shift my body lower to see if I can get his cock back in my mouth, and hover above it. He watches me, lips parted, the lower one swollen and red, tongue heavy. Probably my mouth looks like that, too.

I take hold of his cock with my other hand and start jerking it, slowly, as I expand my hand inside his ass just a little and move it ever so slightly. It pulses in my hand, thicker now, and reddening around the corona. I slide my hand up and down the shaft, his moaning getting louder, his legs starting to kick and push against the bed, against me, against anything he can reach, and I spit into my hand for more lubrication on his cock, sliding easily against the condom. The plastic seems thinner now, like he fills more of it. His asshole pulses and I can feel the ridge of his prostate. I start moving a little faster inside and on his cock, and his eyes roll back, his stomach crunches forward and his shoulders shudder. I feel his cock moving a little more and he comes, yelling out, pulsing under, between, around my hands, pushing his hands up into the wall above his head.

I stroke a little longer, lightly, and ease my hand out of his ass carefully as he quiets, murmuring, "Oh, man, oh, man." I take off the glove and he pulls at the condom, takes the glove from me and tosses it into the small wastebasket next to the head of his bed. I sit beside him and he shifts, puts his hands behind his head, unselfconscious, practically nude, grinning. He really is cute. His cock is already softening and nestles against his leg.

I lean down to kiss him and push his hair back out of his eyes. "So, thanks," I say. "That was fun."

"What'd you say your name was?" he asks, kissing me back. The skin on his chin and cheeks is just a little bit scratchy.

"I didn't say. It's Sinclair."

"Well, thank *you*, Sinclair," he laughs a little, touches my hand. It's sweet.

"I didn't get yours, either."

"Mark."

"Mark," I repeat. Yeah, he looks like a Mark. "Pleasure's all mine, I'm sure."

"I've seen you at the leather night before, haven't I?"

"Yeah, you probably have." I haven't even taken my shoes off, so I don't have to get much together. I walk over to his sink and wash my hands. It's relatively clean in his tiny kitchen, but kind of cluttered, with clean pots and pans stored on the stovetop and no counter space. I dry my hands on the kitchen towel and run them through my hair.

"Heading back there?" he asks. He gets up from the bed to walk me to the door.

"Nah, I'm heading home. Maybe I'll see you there again?"

"Maybe," his eyes twinkle a little, and he smiles, touches my shoulders. "I'd like that."

"A second date already?"

"Well, you know. I'd like the chance to return the favor. If you'd...like that," he dips his head a little again, and my knees go a little weak. He knows; he must know. My hands pulse and I swoon a little, my inner dom soaring happy.

I dig into my pocket for my trick card. "Got a pen?" I ask. He hands me one from his bookshelf which seems to double as his desk. I write *Sinclair* and my email address and hand it and the pen to him, and I lean in to kiss him one more time before heading out the door.

PAGE OF WANDS

Cheyenne Blue

Rose reads my tarot cards under cloudy skies on St. Kilda Esplanade. The Sunday market is in full swing, and Rose's stall is one of many tucked into the confines of the yellow lines painted on the pavement. I'm keeping her company as I often do, killing the time between when I crawl out of bed and the pubs open. Rose is looking more eclectic than usual today; red cotton Indian skirt with a tattered, uneven hem, and a rainbow headband that does nothing to contain her dyed orange hair, which is escaping from an untidy plait to clash with her purple shirt.

She's never read my cards before since I won't pay her ten-dollar fee. I don't believe in this crap anyway, and she's always told me she never reads for free. But today business is slow and the seagulls circling aimlessly overhead outnumber her customers by twenty to one.

She wipes a splodge of seagull shit from the vinyl table and stirs the cards facedown. "Go on, TJ," she says. "Pick a card."

The dare crinkles in the corners of her eyes.

I shrug and pick a card at random.

"Oh-ho." She studies me through narrowed eyes. "The Fool." She flips it back over, stirs the tattered deck with her hands again. "Pick an easier one."

She always says that a battered pack signifies an intuitive and accurate reader. Then she winks, "I let the punters think that, anyway."

Deliberately, I pick one from the bottom and skate it out, flipping several of the cards to the sea breeze.

She glares at me, retrieves them, and studies the card I've picked. "The Page of Wands—someone young, ambiguous of gender. Know anyone who fits that description?" she asks offhandedly.

I have no idea what the Page of Wands is supposed to look like, and I wonder if her comment is deliberate—is it me she's describing? "No," I say, rather too forcefully.

"Then you'll probably get laid tonight." She winks.

"Yeah, right." *Fat chance of that*, I think. Why tonight to break the drought? "So who do I look out for? Doubt I'll meet a movie star in the Espy." The battered old St. Kilda pub is as well known as Luna Park and Melbourne trams. At least it is around here.

"Oh, I don't know." Rose looks pensive. "I once got laid by a bloke I met in the Espy. There was something odd about his dick, though. It was small and had a kink in the middle. Not really worth the effort of dropping my knickers." She shuffles the cards. "Pick another."

I hesitate, and then a potential punter appears in Rose's line of vision. Her voice changes, becomes mellow, deeper, seductive almost. Far different from her normal smoker's croak.

"So make sure you do the lotto, love," she says to me, gathering up her cards. "You might get lucky. And watch out for a mysterious stranger in a red car."

I take the hint and slink off, although I do think she could have come up with something a little more original for my fortune. I see her mouth moving in practiced patter as she lays out the cards for an anxious middle-aged woman, who leans forward and whispers something in her ear.

What secrets Rose must hear.

We meet later for a beer in the Prince of Wales on Fitzroy Street, taking our drinks to the poolroom at the back where the gay boys prance. The barmaid is a tranny with black slashes for eyebrows and bulging, hairy arms. Rose eschews the trendier bar at the front, once the gay boys' domain, now trespassed upon by the yuppie kids who sit at the open windows drinking Chardonnay and watching the parade outside. She says she'll be recognized by her customers. I think she'll be murdered for their money back.

What an odd pair we must appear. Rose so petite and colorful, downright weird looking really, her whole look screaming Wilderness Hippie. And me. Well, I don't exactly scream conservative, with my cropped brown hair and androgynous body and Don't Mess With Me attitude. An attitude that gets me into as much shit as it gets me out of.

I like the Prince because it's as ambiguous as I am. And the clientele here are rather fond of me, too. I can see a couple of the boys looking my way, but they keep their distance because I'm with Rose, and that's just fine.

Rose is complaining about her landlord again. I try to listen, but out of the corner of my eye I can see one of my boys trying to catch my eye. If his pants were loose they'd be wigwammed from his erection; I can see the thick outline of his cock, flattened under the denim. He moves toward the dunny, slowly, so that I can't miss seeing him. I mumble something to Rose, stand

and saunter toward the toilets at the back. The regulars know me well. Sometimes I go into the women's and that means fuck off and leave me alone. Let me drink my pots of VB and brood out over the pool tables. But if I go into the men's...ah, then that's a different story.

I vacillate briefly. Rose is waiting for me; she knows nothing of this, and better that she doesn't. Our friendship is built on fluid lines, but some things have never been defined. However, the promise of fat white cock is a temptation I find hard to pass up. But I can be quick, and he will have to be. Before I can look back to Rose, drawing patterns in the fog on her glass, and change my mind, I enter the men's.

He's in the end stall, as always. "TJ, that you?" His voice squeaks at the end, on the upward inflection. This one tries so hard to be female. He's thinking of having the Operation—you know, the final gender-bender dick decapitation. But right now, it's still all there and still all mine.

I slip into the end stall, where he sits on the can, his pants around his ankles. I lean over him, drop my head down and take him in my mouth. I won't kneel, too bloody subservient, and no one in his right mind would kneel on these floors anyway, they're all streaky with piss from He Who Cannot Aim Straight. And I'm limber, lean and long, an agile skinny streak of nothing; I can twist over and bend down with ease.

I worship him with my mouth and he groans and thrusts up, and lets me caress his fat slug of a dick with my tongue and teeth, lips and mouth. He thickens, grows, lengthens, stretches and I adore the taste of his pale blind cockhead, and the soft skin on his shaft, softer than silk, so sweetly vulnerable. And I fancy I can feel it pulsate against the roof of my mouth as it engorges, throbbing with blood. I lick underneath its proud helmet, run my tongue around that circumcised ridgeline. He tastes sweet, this one; I bet he rubbed his dick with almond oil before he came out today.

I slurp him hard, my reward the salty fluid that seeps from the tip. I push my tongue into the slot, the better to taste him, and I grip his shaft hard. How I love that sweet baby-soft skin, the spongy resilience; how I love his desperation as he thrusts into my mouth. I go slack jawed, letting him set the pace. Then, when he's about to come, I take over again, using suction on the shaft, vibration with my tongue on the head.

He's so vulnerable as he comes, his hips jerking; the thick little pool of semen spills onto my tongue. I straighten slightly and move to kiss him. He's wide-eyed and slack jawed. He's had his little slice of heaven for today, and he kisses me eagerly, tenderly. Oh, how I love my sweet gay boys, how I love their feminine kisses and their masculine bodies.

"TJ, lemme do you," he whispers into my mouth, his hands groping for my crotch.

I move back with practiced ease, evading the seeking hands. I wear my dungarees loose, and I know that they can't sense what's under there, although I know they wonder. Is there a coiled little cock nestled there, or is there moist and dark femaleness, or simply nothing? They'll never know. My body throbs, I'm as aroused as hell, but, as always, I'll take care of myself later. Now, I have to get back to Rose and finish my beer.

"Another time," I say, knowing that like free beer tomorrow, it will never come. I wipe my mouth and slip from the stall, leaving him wide-eyed and grateful, his pants still around his knees.

Rose has finished her beer; I must have been gone longer than I thought.

"Quite some crap you had," she says, matter-of-factly. "Thought you must have died in there."

"It's my shout." I avoid answering her, and go and buy the beers.

I weave my way back to our table the long way, so that I can watch Rose unobserved. She's idly flicking beer mats and catching them, two, three at a time. From a distance they look like her gaudy tarot cards. But it's Rose who I watch; I see the line of her plump white arms underneath the thin purple shirt, the curve of her breast, jiggling slightly as she flips and catches the mats. I see her long, bright braid, wispy with escaping hairs, and the undulating form of her legs, propped up on the other seat, ankles crossed. She doesn't shave her legs and the brown fuzz on her shins makes me want to rub it the wrong way, like I might a cat's, and follow it up under her skirt to see where the hair stops, and then joyfully find where it starts again. I'd like to kiss her mouth, bite her throat and breasts and delve under her skirt with my fingers.

I'd let Rose find out what's underneath my loose clothing, but then I don't know if she would want to.

WHAT I WANT, WHAT I NEED

Jacqueline Applebee

Abigail and me, we were forever. We met at Gay Pride, had a whirlwind romance, toppled into bed and into each other's hearts. We were crazy about each other. We planned on a lovely lesbian wedding, and then we would leave our jobs so we could open up a cake shop. We would see out our years living in a fine old house on the Dorset coast. There would be sugar and cinnamon, love and light.

But Abigail left me. She stole all the money in my savings account. She took Wendel, my stripy cat. A part of my heart was chipped like a bad tooth that needed extracting.

I still had my friends. I belonged to a community of dykes and bitches, sisters and femmes. Even my job at the queer youth community center was good for me, as my colleagues took turns inviting me over for dinner. Things could have been worse, but they would have been even better if the woman I loved had not ripped herself right out of my life.

Zanna took pity on me one Sunday. She popped by my flat

with plastic containers full of West Indian food: curry goat and fluffy white rice. The food was rich and tasty. Little red flecks of chilli peppers exploded on my tongue. I felt that someone in this mixed-up world truly cared for me.

"So, Jenna, when are you gonna end this thing?" Zanna handed me a glass of carrot juice mixed with condensed milk. Orange and white swirls danced in the beaker.

"When am I going to end what exactly?"

"The mourning period. Abigail's gone. That thieving cow ain't never coming back."

"Don't call her that." I took a gulp of my creamy drink.

Zanna clicked her tongue. "You need to get back out there. It's been six weeks. Plenty of good-looking women would love to get their hands on your ass, girl."

Zanna may have been right, but it didn't mean I wanted to listen to her. I looked away, feeling suddenly full. The meat felt heavy in my stomach. She had it easy—her girlfriend had never taken her for what little she owned. Zanna was a strong black dyke. She made her shit work.

Zanna kept on talking. "Why don't we go out tonight? You might get lucky and meet the babe of your dreams."

"I don't think so." I gripped the memories of Abigail in a clenched fist. I didn't want another woman to dull my senses. My pillows still smelled of her perfume. My cunt still faintly tingled from her fingertips. I wiped my mouth with the back of my hand. An orange smear lay over my pale skin. Zanna was a good cook, but Abigail was better. Sure, it had all been veggie, but when a dish was made with love, I could eat it all day long.

Despite my best efforts, Zanna wore me down. My resolve disappeared when she produced some chocolate fudge cake for dessert. She took me out later to our local gay bar. I was pleasantly surprised to see my friends Gary and Bella there, too. Gary had been a volunteer at the London lesbian and gay switchboard for years. He was part of my community's fixtures and fittings. Bella had just started working at a gay bookshop I regularly frequented. She was always patient and friendly when I spent too long browsing the erotic section at the back.

"Jenna, let me get you a drink." Gary flung his arm around my shoulder. "Have you met my cousin, Andy?"

A tubby man I didn't recognize waved at me.

Gary passed me a bright yellow glass—vodka, cloudy lemonade and lots and lots of ice.

I took a sip of the tart drink and leaned closer to my friend. "Is your cousin gay, too?"

"Nah, but he's new to this corner of London. I thought I'd show him the single hot spot." Gary's eyes lit up. "And speaking of hot…" Gary whipped out onto the dance floor and started gyrating against a slim, hairy man.

Bella looked at me expectantly. "Would you like to dance?"

I hesitated for a moment, but then Zanna prodded me in the back. "Sure, why not?" I didn't recognize the tune, but I still remembered how to move my feet. I didn't know Bella as well as Gary or Zanna, but I knew she was nineteen. I felt like a dirty old woman just being next to her. Tiredness washed over me. I slowed my movements. Bella seemed to take that as permission to move even closer. Her juicy tits brushed against my black shirt. My nipples hardened instantly. The taste of lemon was sharp in my mouth. I longed to be touched. It had been six weeks since Abigail had left. No one had held me in that time, save for brief hugs of condolence. I'd barely touched myself either; I didn't fancy a quick wank in the dark. A wave of pure need rose up inside me. I was hungry for warm, living flesh.

I watched Bella closely; she was putting on a show for me.

Everything looked good enough to eat. She would spread her legs for me, no doubt about it. But I didn't want her. Not one bit. My breath caught in my throat.

"Look, I'm just going to go to the bathroom." I scampered away as quickly as I could, but my middle-aged years felt heavy on my frame.

The corridor that led to the smelly toilets was dark, but not so dark that I didn't see Andy as he exited the gents.

"You okay there?" he asked. "You look like I feel."

"It's nothing really," I sighed. "I'm just too old for this crap." I sagged back against the wall, speckled with chipped paint and torn posters for gigs that I had never gone to. "Where's your cousin?"

"Dirty boy got lucky. I went to have a pee and saw him up against the wall with some guy he just met." Andy shook his head. "But how about you? Bella looks like a nice girl."

I shot him a look.

"Oh, I mean, a nice woman."

Andy looked down at his shoes, and then he took a step away, but I touched him on the shoulder. "You're right. Bella is a girl, still a teenager. I don't need a teenager right now."

Andy looked at me evenly. "What do you need?" In the gloom of the corridor, his eyes looked like dark honey.

"I need coffee, fresh air and maybe some chocolate."

Andy grinned. "Let's go." He held out his hand, but I hesitated. I didn't want to walk out of a gay pub with a man. What would everyone think?

"There's a back door just behind you. Let's make a quiet exit."

Andy shrugged his shoulders, and followed me outside. We were sitting in a café twenty minutes later. Tinny Greek music played out of an unseen radio. We sipped coffee that was too strong and ate baklavas that were too sweet. The sugary syrup made my teeth hurt, but I finished off three of the little pastries. Rosewater and pistachios danced around my mouth. I wondered what Andy's skin would taste like if I ran my tongue over his throat. It was just about as far away from the specter of Abigail as I could get before I came full circle.

Andy seemed in a playful mood. "Let me show you something." He took my fork from my plate, and then he jammed it into the table with a twist of his wrist. I jumped a little in my seat, but Andy held up the undamaged fork with a smile. "I've got incredible powers, you know?"

The owner approached our table. "Hey! Do that again," he said, and called out to a clutch of people who had been sitting at the rear of the café. Soon we were surrounded by laughing Greek men. Andy entertained us all with teaspoon bending, and a couple of tricks with disappearing napkins. We got our meal for free.

The owner slapped Andy on the shoulder. "You and your wife come back soon!"

We both froze. What was I supposed to say? Andy and I both hurried silently out into the quiet street. I felt confused. I'd been out as a lesbian since I was twenty-three. Why was I suddenly spending time with a straight man? Why was I enjoying it so much? Had I really been a lesbian at all, or had I been lying to myself for the past twenty years?

Andy seemed to pick up on my strange mood; he stood awkwardly beside me. "Well, it's been a nice evening, Jenna. Walk you home?"

"I don't need you to walk me home," I snapped.

Andy shoved his hands into his pockets. "What do you need?"

I needed to be naked and sweaty. I needed to have some

earth-shattering sex. I looked at him and wondered if I'd said that out loud. Andy's eyes were wide.

We collided in an instant. I pushed him up against a lamp-post. His hands went up my shirt. I gripped his ass. He pinched my nipples. And all that time we kissed with frenzy, smashing lips together until neither of us could breathe.

By the time we made it back to my apartment, I was halfway out of my clothes. We tumbled to the floor as soon as I kicked the front door shut. And yes, being with a man after two decades of only women was certainly different, but different was good. I felt more alive than I had since Abigail. I straddled Andy's lap and rode his sheathed cock like I was at the Derby. He thrust up to meet every slamming jerk I made. My whole body felt electric, and my clit sparkled with pleasure. I gripped his round belly with my thighs, milking out every last drop of sensation. I came loudly and wept with relief.

We finally made it to bed as the summer sun peeked through the windows. However, every time I dozed off, I'd feel Andy's hand on my breast or his erection against my thigh. I wanted to taste him. I sucked his cock, licked drips of precome that oozed from his slit. I discovered a man's body for truly the first time in my life. We fucked until we were both raw and exhausted.

I awoke with a start. My cell phone sang out from the floor. I reached down, flicked it open and sighed. It was Gary.

"Hey, Jenna. I don't suppose you saw where my cousin got to last night? He's got a job interview this morning. My aunty will kill me if she finds out I lost him."

"It's okay," I replied sleepily. "I'll make sure he gets there on time." Even as I spoke, I knew that I should shut the hell up. But my brain and my mouth weren't connected due to the lack of sleep.

"Andy's with you?" Gary almost choked on the words. "What's he doing with you?"

I looked at the phone, guilt making me silent. I passed it to Andy, who had now woken up. After a few whispered words, he jumped out of bed.

"I've gotta go." He passed my phone back to me, shuffled into his clothes and then he was gone.

I buried my face in a pillow once I heard the door shut. There wasn't a trace of Abigail's scent left.

Zanna cornered me at work as soon as I got in a few hours later. I mentally steeled myself as she shut the door to the office kitchen.

"A little bird told me you've been playing away from home."

"Gary?"

"No, actually it was Bella. You really know how to piss a girl off, don't you? She's posting the news all over Facebook as we speak."

My face felt on fire. I didn't know what to say to my friend, but she put a careful hand on my shoulder. "It isn't a crime, you know?" Her voice was gentle.

I was lucky to have a friend like Zanna, but I didn't want to listen. "It is a crime when you call yourself a dyke."

"So call yourself something else." She switched on the kettle.

"Like what? Traitor?"

"Bisexual seems like a good start." Zanna passed me a cookie. She took a bite of hers and grinned. "You know, I used to be married to a man."

"Yeah, but once you became a lesbian..."

"I chose only to be with women, but I still have the occasional feeling for men. I have nice memories of my ex-husband."

I wasn't convinced. "I've heard some stuff about bisexuals. Aren't they all into free love and sitting on fences and shit? Aren't they all confused?"

Zanna shot me a look. "Do you know what you want?"

"Yes."

"Do you know what you need?"

I thought of Andy's low voice and the grunts and pleasured moans he made as he rocked inside me. I definitely needed more of that. But then I thought about gangs of lesbians chasing me with flaming torches and pitchforks. I thought about all the people who probably wouldn't speak to me now that I'd been with a man.

"What about the community?" I almost wailed. "God, I feel like I've let everyone down. I really am sleeping with the enemy."

Zanna rolled her eyes. "Oh, stop your whining, you dozy cow! You're not the first woman to do this. Eat the damn cookie and get on with your life."

I looked down at the cookie in my hand; it was full of chocolate chips, nuts and raisins. I took a bite. Sweetness consumed me.

"Bisexual." I rolled the word around my mouth. "I'm bisexual."

Zanna and I toasted this new revelation with a cup of tea: milk and three sugars.

"So you're bisexual then?" Andy kissed me later that evening.

"Seems that way."

He moved to my tiny kitchen. "Gary gave me an earful when I saw him. He said that he's lost one of the fold, and that I must have turned you straight."

"Gary is mistaken." I was still queer. I was just a different kind of queer now. The possibilities were endless for what I could be.

Andy opened and closed bare cupboards, stuck his head into my mostly empty refrigerator.

"What are you doing?"

He held up a carton of eggs. "Let's have a celebration dinner."

"I don't think bisexuals celebrate coming out." I didn't actually know much of what bisexual people did, even though I worked at a queer community center. I really had no idea.

"I got the job I was after." Andy cracked the eggs into a bowl. "We can celebrate that, too."

I hugged him from behind, and stroked my hands over his crotch. He was hard in moments.

Andy stepped away after a second. "Why don't you cook this up? I got some man's work to do."

My eyes boggled. Man's work? I couldn't believe what I was hearing, but then I grinned as he knelt at my feet. He pushed up my skirt, and inched down my knickers. Andy's thick fingers circled my clit like an expert.

I went up on my tiptoes, and tried to keep the omelette from burning, which wasn't easy as my brain was swiftly melting. I spread my legs wider, clutched at Andy's short hair. Soon his lips replaced his fingers. I came, jerking, holding on to my new lover for dear life.

A few orgasms later, Andy and I settled on my sofa, exhausted but happy. We fed each other fork fulls of eggs. It was a simple dish, but it was made with love. I could have eaten it all day long.

ABOUT THE
AUTHORS

VALERIE ALEXANDER is a writer who lives in Arizona. Her work has been previously published in *Best Lesbian Erotica, Best of Best Women's Erotica, Gotta Have It* and other anthologies.

JACQUELINE APPLEBEE (writing-in-shadows.co.uk) is a black British writer who breaks down barriers with smut. Jacqueline's stories have appeared in various publications including *Best Women's Erotica, Best Bondage Erotica, Penthouse* and *DIVA* magazine. Jacqueline has also penned *An Expanded Love*, a romance about open relationships.

CHERYL B. was an award-winning poet, writer and performer whose work appeared in *Word Warriors: 35 Women Leaders in the Spoken Word Revolution; The Guardian;* Suspect Thoughts; *Reactions 5: New Poetry; Pills, Thrills, Chills and Heartache: Adventures in the First Person.*

LOGAN BELLE is the author of the erotic trilogy *Blue Angel*, published by Kensington, and the erotic romance *Bettie Page Presents: The Librarian* published by Simon & Schuster. Her short fiction is featured in the Cleis Press anthology *Obsessed: Erotic Romance for Women*. She lives in New York City.

CHEYENNE BLUE's erotica has appeared in over sixty anthologies including *Best Women's Erotica, Mammoth Best New Erotica, Best Lesbian Erotica, Best Lesbian Romance, Girl Crazy, Girl Crush* and *Lesbian Lust*. She lives in Australia and is still looking for Rose on St. Kilda Esplanade. Visit her website at cheyenneblue.com.

EMERALD's erotic fiction has been published in numerous print and ebook anthologies as well as at various erotic websites. She is an advocate for sexual freedom, reproductive choice and sex worker rights and blogs about these and other topics at her website, The Green Light District: thegreenlightdistrict.org.

DOROTHY FREED is the pseudonym of an artist turned writer who lives near San Francisco with her husband and dog. She writes both memoir and short stories, and is currently working on a collection of erotic pieces. Her interest in erotica came about because art imitates life.

PENELOPE FRIDAY writes a variety of things. Kind people call her interests eclectic; less kind suggest they are simply bizarre. She gets opinionated in her blog at thecollectivereview. com/penelope-friday.

SHANNA GERMAIN's work has appeared in places like *Best American Erotica, Best Gay Romance, Best Lesbian Erotica,*

Dirty Girls and more. "Speak friend and enter" her dirty, wicked world online at shannagermain.com.

DENA HANKINS has logged thousands of ocean miles as a sailor and even more by air and land. There's nothing sexier than travel and she's intimate with the possibilities, difficulties and pleasures.

TAHIRA IQBAL is a UK-based writer. Visit her website, tahiraiqbal.com, for trailers and credits. You can also check out her erotic vampire short story, "The Queen," in the *Red Velvet and Absinthe* anthology published by Cleis Press.

KAY JAYBEE wrote the novels, *The Voyeur, The Perfect Submissive* and *Making Him Wait*, as well as the novellas *A Sticky Situation, Not Her Type* and *The Circus*. Kay also writes short stories and anthologies for Cleis, Xcite and oystersandchocolate.com. You can follow Kay at kayjaybee.me.uk.

LANE is a *bon vivant* who was writing erotica long before she had any experience of sex to draw from. Sexuality is integral to who she is as a creative force, and even her nonerotic work is sometimes characterized by unmistakably suggestive undertones.

AIMEE PEARL is a kinky bisexual who enjoys the company of bossy guys, enigmatic ladies, and assorted others; and her writing, inspired by her adventures, is more fact than fiction. Aimee's erotic stories appear in *Best Women's Erotica 2010; Longing, Lust, and Love* and *Please, Sir*, among many other places.

Eroticist **GISELLE RENARDE** (wix.com/gisellerenarde/erotica) is a queer Canadian, avid volunteer, contributor to more than fifty short-story anthologies and author of dozens of electronic and print books.

JEAN ROBERTA teaches English in a Canadian university and writes in several genres. Her latest single-author collection of erotica is *Each Has a Point.* Her reviews appear monthly here: eroticarevealed.com. Her posts appear weekly on this six-writer blog: ohgetagrip.blogspot.com.

LORI SELKE lives in Oakland, California. A collection of her erotic stories called *Lost Girls and Others* is currently available from Renaissance Books. More of her work can be found in the anthologies *Ladies of the Bite, Demon Lovers: Succubi* and *The Best of Leatherwomen.*

SINCLAIR SEXSMITH (mrsexsmith.com) runs the *Sugarbutch Chronicles* at sugarbutch.net. Her work appears in the *Best Lesbian Erotica* series, *Persistence: All Ways Butch and Femme,* and *Take Me There: Transgender and Genderqueer Erotica,* among others. She is the editor of *Say Please: Lesbian BDSM Erotica* (Cleis Press, 2012).

SALOME WILDE's fiction appears in such anthologies as Susie Bright's *Best American Erotica 2006* and *X: The Erotic Treasury,* Mammoth Press's *Best New Erotica 10,* and Rachel Kramer Bussel's *Best Bondage Erotica 2011, Gotta Have It,* and, with writing partner Talon Rihai, *Curvy Girls* and *Anything For You.*

JORDANA WINTERS's (jordanawinters.tripod.com) credits include *Gotta Have It, Just Watch Me, Oysters & Chocolate* anthology, *Afternoon Delight, Frenzy, Ultimate Sex, Best Women's Erotica 2008, 2007 & 2006, Sex & Seduction, Uniform Sex* and Erotic Tales, Tassels & Tales, A Woman's Goodnight, Lucrezia Magazine, The Erotic Woman, and Oysters & Chocolate.

NICOLE WOLFE is a writer from northern Indiana whose work has been published in *Best Lesbian Erotica 2010*. She loves travel, cult films, and cute girls of all shapes. "1 Percent Adaptable" is based on a conversation she had with a close friend about bisexuality.

ABOUT
THE EDITOR

RACHEL KRAMER BUSSEL (rachelkramerbussel.com) is a New York–based author, editor and blogger. She has edited over forty books of erotica, including *Anything for You; Suite Encounters; Going Down; Irresistible; Best Bondage Erotica 2011, 2012* and *2013; Gotta Have It; Obsessed; Women in Lust; Surrender; Orgasmic; Bottoms Up: Spanking Good Stories; Spanked: Red-Cheeked Erotica; Naughty Spanking Stories from A to Z 1* and *2; Fast Girls; Smooth; Passion; The Mile High Club; Do Not Disturb; Going Down; Tasting Him; Tasting Her; Please, Sir; Please, Ma'am; He's on Top; She's on Top; Caught Looking; Hide and Seek; Crossdressing; Rubber Sex;* and *Only You.* She is *Best Sex Writing* series editor, and winner of eight IPPY (Independent Publisher) Awards. Her work has been published in over one hundred anthologies, including *Best American Erotica 2004* and *2006;* Zane's *Z-Rated, Chocolate Flava 2* and *Purple Panties; Everything You Know About Sex Is Wrong; Single State of the Union* and

Desire: Women Write About Wanting. She wrote the popular "Lusty Lady" column for the *Village Voice*.

Rachel has written for *AVN, Bust*, Cleansheets.com, *Cosmopolitan, Curve*, The Daily Beast, Fresh Yarn, TheFrisky. com, *Glamour*, Gothamist, Huffington Post, *Inked*, Nerve, Mediabistro, *Newsday, New York Post, Penthouse, Playgirl, Radar*, The Root, Salon, *San Francisco Chronicle, Time Out New York* and *Zink*, among others. She has appeared on "The Gayle King Show," "The Martha Stewart Show," "The Berman and Berman Show," NY1 and Showtime's "Family Business." She hosted the popular In the Flesh Erotic Reading Series (inthefleshreadingseries.com), featuring readers from Susie Bright to Zane, and speaks at conferences, does readings and teaches erotic writing workshops across the country. She blogs at lustylady.blogspot.com.

More from Rachel Kramer Bussel

Do Not Disturb
Hotel Sex Stories
Edited by Rachel Kramer Bussel

A delicious array of hotel hookups where it seems like anything can happen—and quite often does. "If *Do Not Disturb*
were a hotel, it would be a 5-star hotel with the luxury of
24/7 entertainment available."—Erotica Revealed
978-1-57344-344-9 $14.95

Bottoms Up
Spanking Good Stories
Edited by Rachel Kramer Bussel

As sweet as it is kinky, *Bottoms Up*
will propel you to pick up a paddle
and share in both pleasure and pain,
or perhaps simply turn the other
cheek.
ISBN 978-1-57344-362-3 $15.95

Orgasmic
Erotica for Women
Edited by Rachel Kramer Bussel

What gets you off ? Let *Orgasmic*
count the ways...with 25 stories
focused on female orgasm, there is
something here for every reader.
ISBN 978-1-57344-402-6 $14.95

Please, Sir
Erotic Stories of Female Submission
Edited by Rachel Kramer Bussel

These 22 kinky stories celebrate the
thrill of submission by women who
know exactly what they want.
ISBN 978-1-57344-389-0 $14.95

Fast Girls
Erotica for Women
Edited by Rachel Kramer Bussel

Fast Girls celebrates the girl with a
reputation, the girl who goes all the
way, and the girl who doesn't know
how to say "no."
ISBN 978-1-57344-384-5 $14.95

Many More Than Fifty Shades of Erotica

Please, Sir
Erotic Stories of Female Submission
Edited by Rachel Kramer Bussel

If you liked *Fifty Shades of Grey*, you'll love the explosive stories of *Yes, Sir*. These damsels delight in the pleasures of taking risks to be rewarded by the men who know their deepest desires. Find out why nothing is as hot as the power of the words "Please, Sir."
ISBN 978-1-57344-389-0 $14.95

Yes, Sir
Erotic Stories of Female Submission
Edited by Rachel Kramer Bussel

Bound, gagged or spanked—or controlled with just a glance—these lucky women experience the breathtaking thrills of sexual submission. *Yes, Sir* shows that pleasure is best when dispensed by a firm hand.
ISBN 978-1-57344-310-4 $15.95

He's on Top
Erotic Stories of Male Dominance and Female Submission
Edited by Rachel Kramer Bussel

As true tops, the bossy hunks in these stories understand that BDSM is about exulting in power that is freely yielded. These kinky stories celebrate women who know exactly what they want.
ISBN 978-1-57344-270-1 $14.95

Best Bondage Erotica 2012
Edited by Rachel Kramer Bussel

How do you want to be teased, tied and tantalized? Whether you prefer a tough top with shiny handcuffs, the tug of rope on your skin or the sound of your lover's command, Rachel Kramer Bussel serves your needs.
ISBN 978-1-57344-754-6 $15.95

Bottoms Up
Spanking Good Stories
Edited by Rachel Kramer Bussel

As sweet as it is kinky, *Bottoms Up* will propel you to pick up a paddle and share in both pleasure and pain, or perhaps simply turn the other cheek. This torrid tour de force is essential reading.
ISBN 978-1-57344-362-3 $15.95

Unleash Your Favorite Fantasies

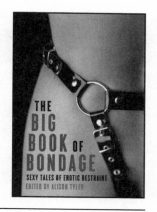

The Big Book of Bondage
Sexy Tales of Erotic Restraint
Edited by Alison Tyler

Nobody likes bondage more than editrix Alison Tyler, who is fascinated with the ecstasies of giving up, giving in, and entrusting one's pleasure (and pain) into the hands of another. Delve into a world of unrestrained passion, where heart-stopping dynamics will thrill and inspire you.
ISBN 978-1-57344-907-6 $15.95

Hurts So Good
Unrestrained Erotica
Edited by Alison Tyler

Intricately secured by ropes, locked in handcuffs or bound simply by a lover's command, the characters of *Hurts So Good* find themselves in the throes of pleasurable restraint in this indispensible collection by prolific, award-winning editor Alison Tyler.
ISBN 978-1-57344-723-2 $14.95

Caught Looking
Erotic Tales of Voyeurs and Exhibitionists
Edited by Alison Tyler
and Rachel Kramer Bussel

These scintillating fantasies take the reader inside a world where people get to show off, watch, and feel the vicarious thrill of sex times two, their erotic power multiplied by the eyes of another.
ISBN 978-1-57344-256-5 $14.95

Hide and Seek
Erotic Tales of Voyeurs and Exhibitionists
Edited by Rachel Kramer Bussel
and Alison Tyler

Whether putting on a deliberate show for an eager audience or peeking into the hidden sex lives of their neighbors, these show-offs and shy types go all out in their quest for the perfect peep show.
ISBN 978-1-57344-419-4 $14.95

One Night Only
Erotic Encounters
Edited by Violet Blue

"Passion and lust play by different rules in *One Night Only.* These are stories about what happens when we have just that one opportunity to ask for what we want—and we take it… Enjoy the adventure."
—Violet Blue
ISBN 978-1-57344-756-0 $14.95

Ordering is easy! Call us toll free or fax us to place your MC/VISA order.
You can also mail the order form below with payment to:
Cleis Press, 2246 Sixth St., Berkeley, CA 94710.

ORDER FORM

QTY	TITLE	PRICE
___	_____	___
___	_____	___
___	_____	___
___	_____	___
___	_____	___
___	_____	___
___	_____	___

	SUBTOTAL	___
	SHIPPING	___
	SALES TAX	___
	TOTAL	___

Add $3.95 postage/handling for the first book ordered and $1.00 for each additional book. Outside North America, please contact us for shipping rates. California residents add 9% sales tax. Payment in U.S. dollars only.

* Free book of equal or lesser value. Shipping and applicable sales tax extra.

Cleis Press • Phone: (800) 780-2279 • Fax: (510) 845-8001
orders@cleispress.com • www.cleispress.com
You'll find more great books on our website

Follow us on Twitter @cleispress • Friend/fan us on Facebook